Short Stories One

By
Theodore Potter

PotterHouse Publishing LLC
Tok, Alaska 99780

DEDICATION

For Fern, My loving and talented wife.

i

ABDUCTION
CHAPTER I

Todd Gram Shaw woke from a deep and dreamless sleep and found himself scared half to death and didn't have any idea why. He never woke up this alert at night. When he did get up in the middle of the night to relieve himself, he was so sleepy; he stumbled to the bathroom and back to bed and never really woke up. Something had made a noise, but what? He threw back the covers just as someone grabbed him. He would have screeched like a stepped on cat, if a large hand wasn't clamped over his mouth. The other arm and hand had pinned both his arms tightly to his body, he was jerked up and pulled in to a bear hug. This scared him so bad he peed all over himself, and down the front of the man who held him. As pee ran down the assailant's front, the man said softly, "Damn". Then he moved over to the window, raised the lower frame, and simply stepped through to the ground outside.

Todd knew he, was being kidnapped and there was nothing he could do about it. He thought of his mother sleeping, unaware her son, soaked with pee, was being taken from his home and would end up no telling where? For some reason he thought about his

Father, whom he only vaguely had memories of. Then the kidnapper stuffed him in a front car seat and released him. Todd scuttled crab like, over to the other side of the car. He seen no point in escaping from this person, he'd only catch him anyhow. The car had been running and was warm inside and soon warmed Todd up and stopped his shivering. Todd noticed the car was new and his abductor had a clean pleasant smell about him and for some reason, this pleased Todd very much. I mean, to be taken from bed by some foul, evil smelling sort, could really mess up ones day, now couldn't it? Todd smiled in spite of the situation he was in.

The new car moved quietly down the street, past Todd's school and under the I-90 overpass then left up the on ramp, going west on I-90. When they were on the Interstate, the man said, "I'm your father. Your mother took you from our home without a word to me. I've looked for you for eight long years of misery and only found where you were two days ago. I'm taking you home to the house you lived in when your mother took you away".

Todd began to weep and didn't know why. He was no longer frightened and knew he was hearing the truth. He had asked his mother quite a few times about his father, but had received only evasive answers. He loved his mom even though he knew she had a few problems, like she drank too much and brought strange men home. Todd had tried to talk to a few of them, but mostly they just didn't respond in any way what so ever.

As the Impala traveled west Todd was quiet for a long time, and then blurted out, "What about my mom? Isn't she gonna be real mad."

Todd saw his father smile by the light of the instrument glow. His father said, "She might be a bit upset, but I think she'll get over it in time. I did. If I had known where you were, I would have come for you at once. Your mother has to deal with the Rapid City Police Department. I reported you missing eight years ago, and they still have an open file on you."

Todd asked, "What about clothes?"

His Dad said, "We will stop when we cross over into Minnesota. We'll go into Rochester, at a   Wal-Martand buy you some clothes O.K?"

Todd Jr. said. "Mom always got my stuff at the thrift store; it'll cost a lot of money at Wal-Mart for new clothes won't it?"

Todd Sr, with a frog in his throat said, "I think I can afford some clothes for you Son."

Todd asked, "What should I call you?"

Todd Sr. pulled over to the edge of the road and looked in his Sons eyes and said, "I'm your Father and you can call me Dad and I'll call you Son, O K?"

There were tears in Todd Sr. eyes, when the boy slid across and into his arms. Both were crying, and the years seemed to slide away. Young Todd had flashes in his mind of a nice home and of his Dad.

CHAPTER 2

As he drove, Todd Sr drifted back in time, to when he had met Todd's mother. Being from North Dakota and a family that really didn't believe in higher education, at least past high school, he wanted more out of life than what his family had planned for him. He became a fulltime student in Spearfish South Dakota; studying economics, while living on Campus. He also worked full time over at Wall Mart, to pay his own way in school. His shift, two to eleven was hard on him,

The only good thing was, he was off Saturdays and Sundays, and if he wasn't too tired on Friday night, he would go down to one of the nightspots and listen to some of the country music being played live there, like the Wilt Brothers playing music at the Silver Spur Saloon, down on Main Street. If he was too tired Friday he almost always made it on Saturday.

One night he was sitting on a bar stool, when a beautiful face appeared close to his and a voice said, "Hello, my name is Ra-chel'." How about you buy me a drink handsome?"

Todd was shy and didn't know how to say no to this beauty, so he bought her a whisky coke and another beer for himself. The girl looked to be about his age and ask, "What is your name?"

He found his tongue and told her; "My name is Todd."

She drank four drinks to his two, one right after the other. Todd knew when he'd had enough and told

Ra-chel', "I must study tomorrow and I'm going home."

She said, "It's too early for me to go home, and I can sleep in on Saturdays and Sundays".

Todd got up to leave and Ra-chel' stood on tip toe and put a lip lock on Todd's mouth that would put a vacuum cleaner to shame. He finally turned away from her and broke the kiss. She said, "I thought maybe, I could change your mind."

Todd knew his face was red and he found words hard to come by. Finally he said, "I would love to stay and party all night, but I simply can't. I'm in third year Accounting and if I don't cram every spare moment, I'll flunk and go home in disgrace!"

Ra-chel' said, "I'm so sorry; I'll give you my phone number, when you find time give me a jingle."

He walked out and never looked back, because he knew if he did, he wouldn't leave. This was as close as he had gotten to social intercourse, since enrolling in this school and he really liked Ra-chel'.

Todd forgot all about Ra-chel', and he lost her phone number anyhow. He thought she might be a bit wild for him. She had belted down six shots of whisky and coke while he had two beers. That was a bit much for the time period.

About three weeks later he was back on the same bar stool, listening to Kenny Cressman tickle the slightly out of tune piano keys through a bunch of easy listening old country songs. Kenny was right in the middle of some song Todd had not heard, since he was a kid, when Ra-chel' popped up between his legs, that he had spread apart in relaxation. She scared the crap out of him and he almost fell off his seat. He said, "Damn! Woman, are you O.K.?"

She retorted with, "Well you didn't call me did you?"

Todd realized he liked this girl, even if she was a bit nuts. He said, "I'm so sorry, but I lost your number and didn't know your last name."

She came back with, "Well its Bonee Pronounced Bo-nay, I come from good French stock, what stock did you come from?"

He said, "I'm part Polish and Scotch and my name's Shaw and I'm third generation and I don't think it makes any difference now anyway."

One month later Ra-chel' announced that Todd Shaw was going to be a daddy, and Todd damn near fainted. He said, "I thought you were on the pill?"

She said, "I am, but I guess it didn't work,"

Todd blurted out, "Just what in hell do we do now?"

Ra-chel' said, "It took the both of us to make this baby and the big decision we must make, is do we keep it or abort it."

Todd felt total revulsion at the idea or even the thought of his child being aborted. He said, "No way in hell are we going to abort our Kid. We'll get married, that's what we'll do! OK?"

Ra-chel' jumped up and into his arms. She said, "Yes, yes, yes!"

They were married in a civil ceremony at the Spearfish South Dakota court house. They ducked classes on Friday and spent all weekend in bed. Todd had vacation time coming from   Wal-Mart so he took the whole week off. They stayed in bed till they were hungry and then went out and ate. Todd knew they were breaking the rules and must find somewhere else to live. They were helped along by a very irate Dean of students. He knocked on their door at seven am Tuesday morning and informed them, they would flat move there asses out and find someplace else to shack up. Just before the dean had his eyes forever crossed by a pissed pregnant French woman, Todd explained to the dean, they were both students at this school and were newly married and didn't see anything to be gained by resorting to name calling and they would be moving out as soon as they could. The dean tried to apologize, but Todd had all he could take from this asshole and waved him away and closed the door in his face.

It was just getting light in the east, when Todd pulled into a best western motel on the out skirts of Rochester, Minnesota. In the room, he told his son, "You might want to wash some of the pee off yourself and then get some sleep."

Todd Jr showered off and wrapped a large towel around himself, then crawled in one of the beds and was instantly asleep. Big Todd took his turn at washing the pee off himself. He donned clean clothing from his bag, and then wrote a note telling Todd he was going to Wal Mart, for a clean change of clothes for him. When big Todd returned, his son was sitting on the bed with the bed covers wrapped about him, reading the note. Big Todd said,"Didn't sleep long did you son?"

Todd replied, "No Dad, I am too excited about all that is happening. It is like; when I woke up I thought I had been dreaming. Now you're back and it's real. I am glad you found me Dad, I love Mom but she drinks a lot, and brings men home all the time. Will I be able to live with you Dad?"

His father said, "For as long as you want son."

CHAPTER 3

Todd came home one night and found Ra-chel' on her lips. A half empty bottle of vodka stood open on the night stand and she was out cold. He took the bottle of vodka to the bath sink and up ended it. He had been afraid of this, he had married an alcoholic. In his heart, he knew he was in for it. He should end it right now. If he just walked out now, he knew he'd never see her again. The only problem was: he loved her and couldn't find the strength to go. He agonized most of the night about it and decided to confront her about trying to kill their unborn child with alcohol. When he woke up his wife was already up and cooking breakfast. When he walked into the kitchen, it was like she hadn't had a drink the night before. He looked at her and asked, "How long have you been drinking a half bottle of vodka at night?"

She set down and looked at him with sad eyes. She said, "That was the first time since we married. With you away working at night, I get lonely and when I get lonely I drink."

Todd told her, "If you so much as look at another drop of booze, before our baby is born, you'll never lay eyes on me again!"

He didn't give her a chance for a comeback; He left and stayed gone all day and into the night. Ra-chel' worried about him and vowed she'd not drink anymore and really meant it.

. CHAPTER 4

Things were in a mess back in Elgin Illinois. When her son failed to respond to her get up call, Ra-chel' went to his room and he was gone. He hadn't gotten dressed however, because his clothing was still on the floor. All he had on was pj's. She ran to the back door with a sinking feeling and looked in the back yard and he wasn't there. She made a mistake then, but wouldn't realize it until much later, she phoned 911 and reported her child kidnapped.

Cops in big batches showed up in a matter of minutes. By that time Ra-chel' knew what had happened to her son; his father had found her and took his son back. She didn't dare tell the police about it either. She was guilty of the very same thing eight years ago and there was no statute of limitations on kidnapping. The police found no evidence of foul play and told Ra-chel,' she should file a missing persons report tomorrow.

When Todd came home that day and found his wife and son gone he sat down and cried for the first time in his adult life. He had convinced himself he was in a solid marriage. He loved his son more than life and had to find them.

He reported the affair to the Rapid City cops, they told him they would put an all-points bulletin out, but don't get your hopes up sir. She could have gone in any direction and would be hard to find.

Weeks went by and no word from the police or Ra-chel'. Todd went half crazy, he couldn't sleep and meat was dropping off him in pounds. His job didn't suffer, instead it became his passion and he threw himself into working. He asked for and received additional accounts in order to keep busy. His co-workers did notice his hollow looking eyes and the weight that stripped off him. His boss; Mr. Hightower came by his cubicle and had a chat with him. He asked, "How are things at home Todd?"

Todd looked at Hightower for a couple of seconds and then made up his mind. He needed to tell someone. He said, "My wife took my son and disappeared a month ago. I hope I'm doing a good enough job for you, I'm worried sick about it."

Hightower said, "You have been doing the work of two or more and losing a lot of weight. Your suit looks like another family moved out of it. I'll tell you what Todd; you need some time off away from here. You have a month's vacation coming. Go to the Caribbean and lay in the sun. Get a girlfriend. It'll make a new man out of you. Your one of my best men and when you get straight, there's an office and promotion for you."

Mr. Hightower got up and left. Todd sat there in amazement, why hadn't he thought of that?

Todd took Mr. Hightower's suggestion to heart and booked an entire month in the south of Mexico. He did get a girlfriend and the ironic thing about it was that she was from Rapid City. Her name was Dawn Charles and the two met on the flight to Mexico. She worked in a bank at home and they were at the same hotel on the same island near Cancun. The two talked each day away and found more than just a few things in common. Dawn only had two weeks' vacation, so Todd cut his short so they could return together. They had just gotten to a point where they were having fun with each other. Todd really liked Dawn, but sensed a hesitation in her as well as in himself. They had both had their hearts broken in previous marriages and neither wanted a repeat of that.

CHAPTER 5

Todd took his new found son shopping, like the boy had never been shopping before. It didn't take him long to get in the spirit of things. The boy's section of clothing really got a work out. By the time they were through, the basket was full and young Todd had a wide eyed look and his heart was singing. He said," I don't see how I'll ever be able to wear all those clothes Dad, but I'll sure give it a try."

Eight years after losing his son he was doing well in his job, in fact he was in line for promotion to General Manager. Mr. Hightower had been promoted to Vice Chair and had picked Todd to fill his old position. When Hightower called him in to tell him, he knocked and was invited in. Mr. Hightower stood and came around his desk and shook Todd's hand, then in a surprise move, led Todd around and sat him down in his chair. He asked, "How does it feel old son?"

Todd had heard rumors and knew what was coming, but tried to look surprised. Hightower said, "I've been bumped upstairs and you have been promoted to fill my slot."

Todd said, "I hope I do you a good job Mr. Hightower,"

Hightower said, "You will Todd and as long as I have you here, I have news for you. We've had an inquiry from I.R.S. Your wife filled a joint tax return and listed you as a dependent and I have her address right here. You're on two weeks' vacation as of now; there's more time if you need it."

Todd was in total shock and looked like he was going to strangle. Mr. Hightower said, "Here man drink some water."

Todd drank all of the glass and set it down hard enough to hurt his ears. He finally found words and thanked Hightower and shook his hand and turned and ran to his office to shut it down. He was gone in five minutes flat. He called Dawn and told her he would be out of town for a few days. She said, "You found them didn't you babe."

He said, "You bet I did honey and I'll call you often O.K?"

They broke the connection. Todd stopped by home and packed enough clothes for a week and tore out on Interstate 90. Elgin Illinois was a long day's drive from here.

CHAPTER 6
Home at last

Todd pulled the Impala in the drive of their home he had gone out on a limb to buy ten years ago. He looked over at his son asleep and thought about the last two weeks. He'd asked Todd if he liked camping out and fishing. Todd hung his head and said," I don't know Dad, I've never been either one, but I'd like to go and find out."

The boy had tears in his eyes and he hugged his son and said, "Son how about I take another week off and we two go camping and trout fishing in the black hills."

The boy let out a yell that hurt his ears and said, "Yes dad, but what do we do about camping gear?"

Todd Sr said, "Well, there's Wal-Mart, we'll stock up and buy all the gear we'll need." That was two weeks ago and the two had a wonderful time. He shook Todd gently awake and said were home son.

Todd was instantly alert and looking at the big house, then he was out of the car and beat his Dad to the door. Todd knew he was back home as soon as he smelled the interior of the house, he ran upstairs and back down again, he went everywhere; just like he did when he was two years old.

Todd Sr. called the police and told them he had found his son and they could close his case. They kept Todd on the line while pulling it up on computer. The Captain came on line and told Todd he should bring his son down to the station and they could sort this thing out. Bells went off in Todd's Head and he retorted with, "You people had eight years to find my son and I'll not bring him out of his home for anyone, you may come and talk to me here if you wish."

Todd hung the phone up without waiting for a reply. Twenty minutes later there was someone at the door. Todd Jr answered the door and yelled, "Dad, the police are here!"

The captain understood then why the father had refused to bring this boy down; the boy was obviously at home. Todd came down and said, "Yes sir what can I do for you?"

The captain asked, "Where did you find your boy, Mr. Shaw?"

Todd replied, "I really do not think that matters now. I don't want to get anyone in trouble. My son wasn't mistreated in anyway, if he had been, I would be the first to stick it to whoever did it."

The Captain was a smart man and knew when he was out gunned, and decided to cut his losses then said, "You're right sir, we'll close the case. You have a good day."

He turned on his heel and went out the door and closed it. Todd was a little disappointed; he was looking for more of a battle.

CHAPTER 7

The very next morning there was a frantic knocking on their door. Todd said, "I'll get it dad."

Todd Sr said, "Whoa son, better let me, I think it might be your mother. I want you to go up to your room and close the door while your mom and I have a nice talk."

The boy nodded his head and took off upstairs. The knocking continued until he opened the door, Ra-chel' blurted out, "Do you have my son here? "

Todd retorted, "I have our son here and good morning to you too."

She asked, "Are you going to let me come in and see him? "

"Not unless you change your attitude". He said, "We can just talk right here."

She said, "Well you could have ask me before you took him in the middle of the night."

"Did you ask before you took him from here eight years ago?" Todd asked. "Hell no, you didn't, and I should never speak to you again, but if you will act civil, I may be able to keep your butt out of jail. It's up to you." He thought that this girl needed a scare put in her. It might help. He added," The cops want to charge you with interstate kidnapping. So far, I refused to give you up, but I'm sure a phone call can get you twenty to life."

Ra-chel' turned white and said, "You wouldn't do that to the mother of your son."

He said, "I don't want to, but if I've got to put up with you hanging around messing up our son's life, then I'll have no choice, will I?"

Ra-chel' began to sob and Todd felt sorry for her and led her in to the kitchen and set her down. He said, "You can only visit Todd here, at least for now. It will be up to you to change that. You need to belong to AA and pull your life together. There's no home here for you."

Ra-chel' between sobs, said she knew she was the one who was wrong and she was sorry and knew that wasn't enough, but she would join AA and pull her life together, she just wanted to see her son sometimes. Todd called his son to come on down. When the boy reached the kitchen door, he hesitated, and then walked over to his mom and into her arms.

Todd went out to his den and let the two talk. He trusted his son, but would never trust Ra-chel' again. After about an hour, his son came and told him his mom was ready to go. Ra-chel' was standing at the door. She said, "I tried to call you a dozen times or more but I would chicken out before it rang and go get drunk."

Todd said with a catch in his voice. "If you had called early on, I would have come and gotten you."

He asked if she had money enough. She looked at him and thought "Damn the booze anyhow." She said, "I had a big yard sale and did real well and I'll get a job in a few days."

She was driving an old Ford car, that had seen better days, but it started right up. Todd said, "Take care Ra-chel' and call before you come around, O.K?"

She said, "Yes I will."

Todd could see tears rolling down her cheeks and it damn near broke his heart. Young Todd was crying too. He came over to his Dad and they hugged for a long time, then Father and Son walked arm and arm into the house.

Theodore Potter

BOOMER
The Haunted Hound

BOOMER - The Haunted Hound
CHAPTER 1

The pup had been acting strange all day and had Darran Buford perplexed. He would lay there peacefully for a time and then jump to his feet and tremble with his hair standing straight up all over his brown and black body. He then would raise his snout to the heavens and emit a howl that was more scream than howl. Each time the dog howled it caused Darrin's hair to stand up on his back and neck. Finally he'd had enough and went to the dog with a leash in his hand. His intention was to lead the animal off in the Tennessee hills out of hearing distance of his cabin. When old Boomer saw him coming with the leash however, he lit out for the surrounding hills like he was scalded. Darran stood there in amazement as Boomer burnt a trail up the side of Lonesome Mountain. Darran wondered why that hound didn't move that fast during a hunt. He had never seen Boomer move like that since he was hatched.

Darran forgot all about old Boomer and got back to attending his moonshine still. He made one good batch a year and drank it mostly himself. Once in a while someone would happen by his remote cabin and if they were female and willing, he would share his stash of moonshine with the gal. This broke down the wall that exists between strangers that chanced to meet way the hell out here.

CHAPTER 2

Way out here was in fact in the northeast corner of Tennessee near the Kentucky line. Lonesome Mountain had belonged to the Buford family for the last three hundred years and since the death of his father five years ago, it now belonged to Darran. He had some papers somewhere that described the property, but didn't much care one way or the other. The mountain was his and everyone here abouts knew it.

Darran was twenty-seven years old and considered to be handsome by the girls. He went to a dance some Saturday nights over in Cumberland Gap and courted all the ladies. Some considered him a good dancer and tried enticing him home with them, but he dodged that and only casually mentioned that the girl might drop up to his cabin sometime. This was more convenient and not as likely to create a lasting relationship.

It wasn't that Darran didn't want a woman about his place on a permanent basis, he just couldn't afford to support another human without going to work and going to work meant moving to town thirty miles away from his beloved cabin. His father had built this place before he was born and his earliest memories were of crawling about the polished floors or scooting about on his butt and then learning to walk while hanging on to one of the pet dogs. The walls were squared hardwood logs, dove tailed and cemented in place. It was known as the three hundred year house in these parts and Darran had no doubt that it would make it.

CHAPTER 3

Darran had gained an education through his mother who had been a teacher when she met his father out in Virginia, back before the big war. When she saw the mountain, she fell in love with it and declared she wanted to have a child and teach it only. Buford Senior did his part and impregnated Delsey Mai with Darran and by the time Darran was four he could read and spell as good as any third grader. When he was thirteen his mother took sick and died within two short weeks. The two Buford's almost went crazy with grief at her loss. Buford Senior took to moonshine in grief and it was downhill from the start. He lasted for a year and Darran found him dead one cool morning and was thankful his father wouldn't have to suffer any longer. Both his parents were buried in the family burial plot on the fringe of the back yard. It took him two years to heal up from his double loss. Now he was content just to be alive and able to enjoy it.

CHAPTER 4

Darran jumped to his feet and couldn't remember what woke him, until he heard such a god awful scream that he broke out in chills all over his body and wanted very much to jump back in bed and pull the covers over his head. The scream was coming from his back yard near where his mother and father were buried. He looked out into the moon lit yard and saw old Boomer digging at one of the older graves. Yep old Boomer was digging and screaming at the same time. Then Darran gasped and almost pissed his pj's, because there were two wispy white ghost figures standing watching Boomer dig. When Darran saw this, he let go with an involuntary screech and the two figures disappeared in an instant. Old Boomer stopped digging and lay down beside the hole he had made and went fast to sleep. Darran found himself trembling all over and sat down on the bed with his head in his hands. Hell, he had a haunted dog on his hands. Now just what in hell did one do with a haunted dog? He supposed if he shot it, it might come back and haunt him.

The two ghosts had been a man and a little girl and had been holding hands. What had happened to make them haunt his pup, he had no idea. He needed to check the name on the head stone when daylight came. He had no intention of going out in the night after seeing those ghosts.

He couldn't get back to sleep real soon and when he finally did, he was woke up by Boomer scratching at the door to be fed. He went to the door and old Boomer tried to come in, but he stank to high heaven and Darran slammed the door in the dogs face. Boomer looked like he had been in the outhouse hole all night and smelled much worse. No way could he come in the house. Boomer went and lay down as Darran filled his bowl with dry dog food and slipped it through the crack of the door. Boomer ran over and consumed it with gusto, then went to the watering trough and drank his fill. He seemed normal; maybe the haunt was over.

Darran was about to freshen up the fire under his mash, when Boomer let go with even a more horrendous screech. He ran outside of his barn and there was old Boomer digging and screaming away. Darran didn't see any ghostly figures, but he reasoned they would be invisible in daylight. They must have disappeared when he made a noise, because old haunted Boomer flopped down and went to sleep. Darran thought he must do something, this was too nerve wracking to suit him.

CHAPTER 5

The name on the grave read General Seyrous Darran Buford; his great granddaddy. This great grandfather had been a General in the American Colonies in the war against the Brits. He had been given Lonesome Mountain to compensate for his service to his country. There were mutterings among the family that the general was somewhat of a fake and didn't deserve the mountain. This really didn't matter to Darran one whiff. The deed said it was his and that was that. He wrote the dates off the head stone and fired up his old Ford and drove to the county seat over in Harrogatt, Tennessee. The town was a sleepy little burg and not very busy. He parked at the courthouse and went in. The lady at the front desk nicely asked him if she could help him. Darran asked her where he could find out about how folks that were dead had died. The ladies eyes got as big as saucers and she became nervous. She said, "The records department is on the second floor, take those stairs right over there."

He did as he was told and found a much younger female at a desk near the entrance. She smiled at Darran and said, "Well hello there you good dancer you."

Darran recognized her as one of the dance partners he had danced with a few times at the Gap. Her name tag read Jenean Bowers. He said, "Well thanks for the complement, I happily return it. You dance well yourself Jenean."

Jenean asked him what she could do to help him. He looked at this girl and liked what he saw and he needed to talk to someone about what was going on out at his place. He decided to come clean with her. He asked, "Do you have time to listen to something?"

She perked right up and said, "Oh yes I do Darran."

He thought hell; she knows my name, that's interesting.

As Darran unfolded the story about old Boomer's antics, Jenean's eyes got bigger and bigger. When he produced the name of his grandfather; Jenean grabbed it and all but run back to a computer. She began typing furiously on the key board. Soon she stood and waited for a printer to print out a document. She handed it to Darran and said, "That's all there is to tell you what happened to your great grandfather Seyrous back when he died.

The story was short and sweet; the General had challenged a Jerrod Whimbly to a duel and lost the damn thing while losing his life to boot. Seems this Jarrod had come to town and insulted the general in some way that wasn't at all clear to this day. The General had felt his honor was at stake and had foolishly accepted the tossed out bait and got his ass shot off. That was all the article provided in the way of information. Darran told Jeneane he was grateful for her help and said his goodbyes. Jenean looked like she wanted to lock up the damn place and go with him. Darran liked her and said as he parted,

"Why don't you drop by my place this evening and have a bite to eat."

Jenean bobbed her head and gushed, she would just do that.

CHAPTER 6

Darran had an uncle named Rufus Buford, who was a bit on the crazy side and had a reputation to match. He was somewhat clairvoyant, in so far as that when he had about half bottle of moonshine in him, he saw things that no one else did. Rufus was his father's older brother and Darran would rather be beaten with a crap house pole, than to visit with him, but he needed some answers and knew of no one better than crazy Rufus to get them from.

Darran had gone to visit his uncle when his mother had passed on and got the shock of his life. His cousin Delphie Jane was the same age as he and about as ugly a human specimen as there was on this earth, however she had a body that most women only dreamed about and went about mostly scantily clad in rags. When Darren had stopped his car that day, he was almost dragged out of it by Delphie and rushed to the barn, where he lost his virginity many times over. He slunk back to his car and drove erratically back home. He had been hurting in so many places he had a hard time getting up from bed the following morning.

He recalled all this as he parked in his Uncle's drive. He knocked on the door and heard footsteps coming. The door was jerked open and his Uncle stood there with a wild look in his eyes. He yelled, "Just what in hell do you want boy?"

Darran almost ran, but said instead, "I'm your Nephew Darran, Uncle Rufus."

Rufus looked long and hard at Darran and then said, "Well come on in Nephew and have some dinner with me."

His Uncle turned on his heels and went to the kitchen. Darran followed him and stopped when he saw Delphie setting there at the table. Delphie grinned at Darran and said, "Hey Cousin how's things."

Darren wanted to run once more, but edged on over to the table and sat down. Delphie stood up and went to the stove and returned with a plate with some greasy looking mess covering it. Darran wasn't hungry anyhow and felt nauseous from the smell coming from the stuff. He figured he better make a plausible excuse if he wanted some information from his Uncle Rufus. He picked the plate up and handed it back to Delphie with the explanation, that he had just eaten in town and would she please forgive him. Delphie had a hooded look as she took the plate back and walked to the sink.

Rufus took all this in and asked his nephew what brought him here today. Darran asked him if he remembered much about his grandfather Seyrous Buford. Rufus reared back in his chair and said with vehemence, "That damned old fake was a sorry piece of crap and was run out of Washington just ahead of a lynch mob. He was given Lonesome Mountain to keep him here in Tennessee and out of Washington. He killed some people back there, just to watch them die. The man that he challenged and lost to was a survivor of one of the families that he beheaded. He thought it great sport to raise hell with the poor farmers that were of English decent and with his men, plundered many farms, robbing and killing what he referred to, as the Brit bastards. The Brit that finally killed him was a brother of one of the families he and his men had plundered and killed down on the Virginia coast. The man had arrived in America, intending to visit with his long lost relatives, only to find them all dead. When he sought out the truth, he made a beeline for Lonesome Mountain and flat killed the damn General in a dual."

CHAPTER 7

Darran got the hell out of there before Delphie could steer him to the barn. It wasn't that she didn't try, it was that Darran moved too fast for her and when she made it to the porch, he had the old Ford wound up headed for home. Darran thought damn, if that cousin wasn't so damned hard to look at he might be more interested in her, but they were first cousins and likely to have a two headed kid or something and that wasn't too cool.

There was a late model Chevy Cavalier sitting in his drive, containing one Jenean Bowers, when he pulled into his drive. This gal was serious as hell. He suddenly had a premonition and almost backed out and run away, but she was a cute thing and he decided this outweighed the risk of consorting with her. He killed the Ford and got out. Jenean exited her car at the same time and they met halfway. She came right in his arms, catching him off guard. All he could do was hug her in return, what the hell. They made small talk as they went in the house. Jenean said, "You have a beautiful home here Darran."

He thanked her and went to the kitchen for drinks, after making her comfortable in the living room. Out in the kitchen, he put together a concoction of part moonshine and part coke. The moonshine was of his own making and was good enough to drink straight; however, he only wanted to get her a little intoxicated; not falling down commode hugging drunk, hell there would be no fun in that.

Jenean took a sip and brightened up and said, "That's really nice! What is it?"

Darran replied with, "I make my own once a year and this stuff is four years old. I store it in oak casks out in the barn."

The party carried on for the rest of the evening. The two enjoyed talking to each other and prepared a meal together as well. When bed time rolled around there was no discussion about it, they simply went to bed and made love.

CHAPTER 8

At three in the morning old Boomer did his thing and literally scared the crap out of both Jenean and Darran. They grabbed each other and hung on for dear life. Darran was the first to recover any normalcy and ran to the window. The same two ghosts were encouraging Boomer to dig at the general's grave. When Jenean saw this she flat peed her panties and let go a scream that must have been heard all the way in town. Jenean's scream completely un-nerved Darran and caused his bowels to gurgle. The two ghosts disappeared in a flash and filthy old Boomer stopped his wailing and fell asleep right where he was. Jenean and Darran held each other in the dark, while trying to come to terms with what they had been witness to.

Darran and Jenean talked about it all night, not going back to sleep until seven am. They slept until almost noon. Jenean jumped up and said, "O my god! I'll bet you I don't have a job now. I was supposed to be at work at nine."

Darren's heart sank, he knew he was responsible for this and knew his life had just changed forever. He said, "Well it's too far to drive to a job in town from here anyhow."

Jenean stopped dressing in mid bra installation and gazed at him. She slowly sat down on the bed with one beautiful breast hanging out and asked him, "Are you saying what I think you're saying dear heart?"

Darran bobbed his head and Jenean tossed her bra on the floor and fell into his arms. The two wanted to consummate the deal right then and there.

It would have happened too, if ole Boomer hadn't been re-haunted at that moment. The horrible screech he let go of, drove all desire from the two lovers and both jumped out of bed onto the floor. Darran said, "Damn, maybe we both should get the hell out of here."

Jenean responded with, "Why don't we go see your uncle you talked about, maybe he can tell us what to do."

The thought of seeing Delphie again, caused Darran to hesitate for a moment, but he knew she was right and he had some protection from his oversexed cousin with Jenean being by his side. He said, "Let's dress and get the hell out of here babe, I can't stand much more of this crap. Let me scare the two ghosts off, so ole Boomer can get some rest."

Darran went to the back door and after throwing it open, yelled, "Get the hell away from my dog ghost." What happened then was really scary; the ghost must have been surprised, because some force Darran didn't see knocked him flat on his ass on the floor. The windows rattled all over the house and the sound of things being dragged about the attic came down through the ceiling. This caused both Darran and Jenean to scuttle out the open door and bolt to the cars out front. Boomer sat quietly at his dig and watched the two weird acting humans running to a car and speed off down the road. After they were gone, Boomer lay down and went to sleep.

At his Uncles house, Darren pulled in and sat for a minute to collect himself. Jenean asked if he was ok. Darran turned to her and decided to fill her in on his cousins over active sex drive. When he finished, Jenean was in stitches. Darran laughed with her and knew this was a good person and probably would be with him a long time.

They approached the house with hearts melded together and damn near tripped over Delphi's legs. She had been laying in wait for Darran, but after seeing Jenean, tried to make her escape by crawling into the bushes. She didn't quite get turned around in time and her bottom extruded out on the pathway. Darran thought damn; his cousin had one hell of a bottom too. Jenean become tickled at the ridiculous situation and Delphie got mad, got up and stomped off somewhere back of the house. Darran and Jenean knocked on the door. His Uncle Rufus yelled for them to come the hell in and stop beating on his door. Jenean found that funny as well and when Darran opened the door, she was still laughing. Rufus looked at her and said, "Just what in hell do you find so funny girl?"

Jenean retorted with, "You sir, that's what."

Rufus sit down hard on his chair and cocked an eye at her. He said, "And just who in hell are you, wise ass one?"

Jenean came right back at him by saying, "The girl that loves your Nephew that's who."

Rufus said, "Well come on over here and give your new Uncle a hug wise ass one."

Jenean laughed and did just that. Rufus said, "Nephew you really know how to pick em don't you boy."

Darran grinned and said, "Yep sure do Uncle."

Rufus said, "What can I do to help you two?"

Darran decided to tell the whole truth this time and fell to it. After he finished his Uncle said, "Son-of-a-bitch. That old bastard is being haunted by some of his past deeds isn't he boy, those ghosts you saw are more than likely two of the people he killed long ago and they are unable to cross over until justice is done."

Darran said, "Well I think you're right Uncle, but what do we do about it?"

Rufus asked him, "What's this we shit boy? That ghost isn't haunting one of my dogs now is it?" He said, "The big question is what are you going to do about it buddy?"

Darran said, "Well I was hoping you could give me some pointers on how to go about it Uncle."

Rufus was silent for a spell and then he said, "You have got to dig up that old man's bones and retrieve his sword that he probably used to behead the two ghosts with, I've heard of this before. If you rebury the sword, the ghost may well enter the new grave and you will get rid of them."

Darran had hoped for some less labor intensive way to solve the problem, but he supposed he had better try it anyhow.

CHAPTER 9

When they arrived back at the cabin all was quiet. Old Boomer was half starved and smelled dead so Darran set his food out through the crack in the door. Boomer ate it so fast he almost choked. He was one hungry hound. Darran and Jenean had lunch and a love break. This time ole Boomer remained complacent and the two had wonderful sex that tore the bed clothes all to pieces.

The howl began low, but escalated in volume until it was as loud as a freight train whistle. Darran tried to pull the covers over his and Jenean's head but, Jenean hit the floor running. Darran got up and looked out the window at the grave site. There were four ghosts out there now and all were egging old Boomer on at his digging. Dirt was flying ten feet high behind Boomer and he was screaming at full volume. The other two ghost were girls in their teens. They were twins and had been beautiful when alive. Darran thought boy o boy, we are in deep pooh now. He went out the front of his cabin and around to the shed. He entered and came back with two shovels. As he rounded the cabin the four ghosts dissipated into thin air. Boomer whimpered and fell to the side and was sound asleep instantly. Darran handed one of the shovels to his new partner in life, with an apologetic look and said, "Not much of a honeymoon sweetheart but, we'll have no peace or get a piece until this bunch of ghost are put to rest."

Jenean got so tickled at him that she sat down on the ground. She had always liked Darran, but now was beginning to realize what a good man he really was.

CHAPTER 10

They dug for the better part of the day and finally got down to a casket. When they hauled it out it was surprisingly light and when set on the ground seemed still intact after all these years. Darran opened the casket door and saw a military uniform that was mostly rotten along with some bones. There wasn't any rotten smell, but a musty smell hit them both and made them back up. There was a military sword laying in a rotten scabbard on the general's right side. Darran reached down and pulled the sword out. It was in beautiful condition and had gold inlayed diamonds at its hilt. Darran couldn't help think that this thing is worth some money. He wasn't about to mess with it however, he just wanted to do the right thing and get these damn ghosts to hell out of here, so ole Boomer would stop being haunted. He stuck the sword in the mound of dirt next to the grave and both moved inside the cabin. He knew what had to be done, but it was more work than he could do in one day; hell he was going to be sore as a stubbed toe now. He told his newly acquired girlfriend, they should go to town and enjoy a movie or something. Jenean agreed whole heartedly and the two took off to town in his ford.

CHAPTER 11

Jenean directed him to her parent's house near the railroad. She wanted to introduce Darran to her mom and dad. Jenean's father wasn't home, but her mother was there and as sweet as any mother could be. Her name was Jelsey May and impressed Darran by the way she took the news that her daughter had fallen in lust with him and said the hell with her job. She said, "I don't think your father will be too happy, but you are of age and must do what you must do, so don't take his ravings too serious."

Jenean told her mother she would be living with Darran out at the cabin and would get to town as often as possible to see them. The two were just about ready to leave when Ray Bowers showed up. He was introduced by Jelsey as Janean's new boyfriend. Ray Bowers had worked hard all his life on the railroad and been retired for a year now. He looked at Darran and must have liked what he saw. He took Darren's hand and said, "If you do her wrong, there won't be any place for you to hide."

Darran croaked out, "Thank you sir, thank you."

He was near crapping himself. This man stood six-foot-seven and weighed in at over three hundred pounds and there was no fat on his frame. He could easily break every damn bone in his body. He might just have to marry this girl, if she would have him that is.

After they made their escape Jenean said, "My dad is an old softy and he likes you, so don't worry, we're ok."

Darran knew somehow she was right. He had in some way been handed a golden pass to a happier life. He was walking on air as they made their way to his ford. Jenean told him she needed to pick up some clothes before they returned to the cabin. Darran told her it might as well be right now. Jenean went back in and ten minutes later came out with a packed suitcase. The die was most definitely cast now, he had a moment of reflective thought, but it passed instantly and he was fine again.

CHAPTER 12

After a movie that wasn't any more interesting than their life was, Darran drove the thirty miles to the cabin. All was quiet as the two new lovers parked in the drive and listened to the night sounds of Lonesome Mountain. Just as they were about to move from the car to the cabin, a light lit up the night sky behind the cabin. Darran whispered let's be super quiet and sneak in the house. They didn't even fully lock the doors on the Ford and silently slipped in the house. Both went to the window and peeked out. Ole boomer was sitting peacefully near the casket, while four ghosts were grouped about the sword stuck in the berm of dirt next to the graves they seemed to be trying to extract the sword from the dirt, but it wouldn't move for them. Darran decided to leave them alone and just take his new love quietly to bed and go to sleep. He preferred not to repeat what took place when he had stuck his nose in where it didn't belong and caused such a ruckus the day before and besides, his ass end was still sore where he had landed on it.

CHAPTER 13

The morning came peacefully and quietly. Darran and Jenean came awake slowly and both felt fully rested. Darran got up and after attending the bathroom {out house} put coffee on to perk. Jenean went to the outhouse and returned to the kitchen stretching and yawning. To the both of them, it felt like they had been together forever and were very comfortable with each other. As Darran was pouring coffee in a cup, old Boomer let go with a screech and caused him to miss the cup with a good amount of coffee. He sat the pot on the stove and went to the door. The sight took his breath away. Old Boomer had the sword in his mouth and was trying to drag it off. The only problem was old Boomer had never dragged anything off in his life before and didn't have a clue as how to do it now. He more or less hung on to the sword and screamed. Boomer looked half dead and made Darran do what he had swore he wouldn't do again. He yelled, "Hey you people or whatever you are, let that pup have some peace and quiet."

The reaction was swift. Old Boomer fell into the hole and went to sleep and expecting some force to zap them both, Jenean and Darran ducked down behind the door and waited for the crap to fly. The first thing was that the door was ripped completely off its hinges and splintered to smithereens. The entire cabin began to shake and rattle. The timbers creaked and moved about and if it hadn't stopped when it did,

Darran was sure the cabin would have been destroyed.

All of a sudden it was deathly quiet. Darran and Jenean held each other and came slowly to their feet. Darran thought damn, we have got to bury that sword somewhere before the bunch of mal-aligned ghost tore his beloved cabin completely down. Jenean looked like maybe she shouldn't be here any longer. Darran told her maybe she should go and spend the day at her mom's, while he tried to help these miss-a-lined puff balls of ghosts cross over to the other side. He said, "I couldn't stand it if you got hurt out here."

Jenean didn't have to think about it twice, she was clothed, kissed goodbye and out the doorless back door in five minutes flat. Her little Chevy screamed down the road and left Darran feeling lonesome for the first time in his life since his mother died.

CHAPTER 14

When Jenean told her mother and father what was happening out at Darren's place they were aghast that she had deserted Darran. Her dad said, "Write some directions down and pack me a lunch for two, I'm going out there and help Darran."

The two women jumped to it and Ray Bowers went out the door and drove like mad for the thirty miles to Darren's place. Ray took the place in in one long look and thought maybe his daughter had made a good choice in selecting this man as her partner in life, not withstanding a few ghosts.

Darran heard Ray's truck pull up and went out to meet him. Ray shook Darren's hand and told him he was sorry he had been so stern with him the day they met at his home and he was here to help if he could. Darran took a liking to this mountain of a man and invited him in. Ray took in the shattered door laying ten feet from the house and whistled and said, "Boy oh boy, these ghost friends of yours are making a mess of your nice cabin son. What do we have to do to put the quietitous on them?"

Darran looked at Ray and answered with, "Put what on them?"

Ray laughed and said, "That's slang for putting a stop to their antics permanently."

Darran said, "Oh, now I understand and I was told by my Uncle Rufus that I would have to rebury the ghost someway and the only way I can think of is to hold a mock funeral and rebury the sword along with the ghost."

Ray asked, with an incredulous look on his face, if he really thought that might work. Darrin's face grew red and he came back with, "Well do you have any better idea Mr. Bowers?"

It was Ray's turn to get red in his face and he realized this boy had his act together and just maybe it would work after all. He said, "Let's find somewhere away from your house and dig a grave son, what do you say to that?"

They smiled at each other and Darran went around the house to the shed and came back with his pair of shovels. They looked down at Boomer and saw that he was curled up at one end of the grave, sound asleep. Darran told Ray they should leave him there for the time being. He picked up the sword and he and Ray walked up Lonesome Mountain till they got tired and stopped then rested at a level spot in a nice small meadow. Darran thought hell; I wouldn't mind being buried in this beautiful place. After he and Ray stopped breathing so hard, from their walk up the mountain, they lit into digging a standard grave hole. The dirt was soft on top, but soon become dry and a bit hard to dig, Ray saved a lot of work simply because of his weight. When three hundred plus pounds landed on a shovel, something had to give and in this case, it was dirt. Soon they both were sweating like crazy. The June weather was warm up here. They took a break and were just settling down when they heard ole Boomer coming up the trail and he sounded like some demon let loose.

Ray had never heard Boomer and almost peed himself and was getting to his feet and preparing to defend himself. In all his fifty-two years he had never heard anything like this and it caused his bowels to loosen considerably. He looked at his companion and asked, "What the hell is that son?"

Darran almost laughed, but he was scared witless as well. Boomer broke out of the brush and went straight to the sword and attempted to pick it up in his teeth. He did all this while screaming loud enough to hurt the human ear. Darran knew the ghosts were present and haunting old Boomer, you just can't see them in the bright sunshine.

Darran motioned to Ray that they should retreat down the mountain and let Boomer have his way with the sword. Hell he couldn't move it before, so probably wouldn't do it now. Back at the cabin they found Darren's Uncle Rufus and Delphie sitting in Rufus's old truck in the drive. Rufus said, "Boy I thought maybe you could use some help removing those haunts from your dog. What have you done so far?"

Darran was wary of Delphie because she was so scantily clad that she was even making Ray eyeball her half necked body with some lust in his eyes. Hell he supposed even Ray was human at that and if you got past her ugly, the rest of her looked like a playboy center fold.

Darran told his Uncle what he and Ray had done so far. Rufus sat there and thought about it for a spell, then spoke, "You have got to have a casket that closes tight so that when you put the sword in it the ghost go in as well. Then when you bury the thing those ghost will be six foot under and shouldn't mess with your pup anymore. I'll go to town and get a box made with a tight lid."

He backed out and drove off with Delphie looking lustfully at both him and Ray. Ray sat down on the front porch and said, "Son-of-a-bitch, that girl has one hell of a body on her do you know that son."

Darran said, "Yeah once you get past her face that is."

Ray grew red in the face and stated he hadn't even looked at her face, there was too much to look at otherwise. Both men had a good laugh and knew they would be friends now for sure.

Darran and Ray were spent and couldn't imagine going back up that mountain today. After a while they ate the lunch Jelsey had packed for the two. Now when Jelsey packed a lunch she didn't take any shortcuts, Ray was a big man and ate like a horse, Darran on the other hand was a fairly light eater and was satisfied long before Ray got fully started so he went out to the barn and pulled a gallon of his four year old stuff from the oak cask, it mellowed in. Back in the cabin he poured up two small glasses full and handed one to Ray. Ray took a sip and declared it to be great stuff. Ray cautioned him, that it had the kick of a mule and would make him unable to scratch his own ass, if he consumed too much too fast.

About two glasses later, sure enough Ray, not being used to his moonshine, was rip roaring drunk. Darran cut him off before he went completely under and Ray hit his couch and was snoring loudly when Darran lay down on his bed and went fast asleep

CHAPTER 15

A pounding on the front door woke Darran up from a deep sleep. He hit the floor still groggy and stumbled to the door and flung it open. There was Delphie with even less clothes than before, if that was possible. He stared at her like she was some lower form of life and then realized who she was and felt ashamed of himself. He told her to come on in and make herself at home. Rufus came in behind her and went straight to the kitchen and the gallon of moonshine. Darran thought, oh damn; now there would be hell to pay. His Uncle had a reputation for drinking and always became surly after a few too many. He had heard tales, but had never actually witnessed it first hand and wasn't looking forward to it now. He got Ray in tow and told him they needed to drive to town and leave his wild ass Uncle here with his oversexed daughter. What was about to happen wouldn't be a pretty sight. He told his Uncle to make himself at home and he and Ray would be back shortly. Rufus was stuck in to the moonshine now and didn't much give a good crap what his Nephew did or didn't do. When he saw that his Nephew was really leaving, he grabbed the jug and followed them out to Ray's truck. He said, "If you leave we are going home now."

He and Delphie jumped in the old Ford truck and he backed out onto the road. Darran couldn't help noticing his jug of moonshine went home with his Uncle and Delphie.

Darran stopped when the two drove off and asked Ray if he would mind going on back and telling Jenean it was safe to come home. Ray said, "I sure will and I'll come back tomorrow and help you get that box your uncle dropped off, up the mountain."

Darran thanked him for his help and went inside. He was still tired, but couldn't sleep right off and lay there thinking about things. Finally he got up and went to the barn and found an almost new piece of half inch plywood. He nailed it over the door hole and felt more secure. As he finished, Jenean drove up with her car full of all she must own in the world. Darran and Jenean hugged each other and declared they both missed the other. They unloaded the car and put the things in the living room. Jenean said, "There are some things I don't need in this mess, but my mom wanted me to have them and I didn't have the heart to refuse her."

Darran laughed and told her he understood.

CHAPTER 16

They were awakened by Boomer scratching at the plywood. In his mind the door had turned solid and now he would probably starve to death. He had been fed all his life at that back door and needed some food now. Darran took the bag out the front door and around to the back. He poured a goodly amount in Boomer's food bowl and stood back watching him eat. Old Boomer was looking poorly and if this haunting didn't cease soon, he would die. Darran heard Ray's Ford truck pull up and park. He walked around to the front and said, "Good morning sir, how are you today?"

Ray said, "Sore as hell, hung over and ashamed of my wicked thoughts about your half necked cousin, that's how I am."

They both cracked up with laughter until they noticed Jenean gazing with reproach at them from the door way of the cabin, they both were embarrassed and coughed into their hands and tried to get real busy, real quick. Jenean smiled and went back inside. Ray looked peevishly at his friend and said, "We almost got me in a lot of trouble son and that I don't need at my age.

Darran said, "Hear, Hear sir."

CHAPTER 17

The two men picked their way up the side of the mountain to the new grave site lugging the big plywood box that would double for a casket along with them. They had to stop several times on the way to catch their breath. When they got there, old Boomer was laying on the mound beside the sword sound asleep. The hole they had dug the day before was too narrow for the box Rufus had had built in town and they fell to making the hole bigger. This proved to be almost as hard as digging the hole in the first place. Old Boomer woke up and watched the two men work. He stank to high heaven and Darran was glad the wind was blowing his smell away. Just as the two men were about finished in the hole, old Boomer let go with a heart freezing screech and grabbed a hold of the sword, and attempted to drag it off. Ray Bowers bolted up and out of the hole and was moving with a speed that defied his weight and height and was hell bent down the mountain at full tilt. Darran followed at a much slower pace. Hell he was flat pooped out and not too worried about the ghosts and ole Boomer. He arrived at the house and found his friend Ray panting like a leopard. He said with much gesturing of his hands that, "By damn that dog and those ghosts scared me half to death and i don't know just how much i can stand of their crap."

Darran told him if he didn't want to, he didn't have to go up there anymore. He wouldn't blame him one bit. He would sneak up tomorrow and put the sword in the casket and hide out of sight until the ghosts went in, then close it tight, so not one of them could escape. He supposed in theory it might work, but he didn't have faith in what he had to do and wasn't looking forward to doing it either.

Ray looked at his daughter's choice of a man and retorted, "You don't think I'm going to desert you now do you son?"

Darran returned his look and said, "I was hoping you felt that way Pop and then shook his hand."

Ray felt pride that this boy had called him Pop. He supposed he had gained a son in this deal.

CHAPTER 18

Darran told Jenean they should go to town and get a real door for the back of the cabin. He measured the hole and then followed Ray down the road. Town was a busy place on a Friday night and the lumber yard was bustling. Darran told the clerk what he needed and was led to doors leaning on a wall. He found the right one and was out of there in five minutes flat. He asked Jenean if she felt like a movie and she smartly came back with, "I don't know if I do or not." as she ran her hands up and down her front. Darran lost it then and set down on the curb and laughed his butt off. He needed this and it made him realize how much fun this girl was. He drove straight home and went straight to bed and made love to his girl.

CHAPTER 19

Ray arrived early the next morning and drank coffee with his two kids. He had talked with his wife the night before and both agreed that Darran was a good candidate for a son-in-law and decided to help the situation along as often as was prudent. Darran said, "Well Pop this is the day. I think we ought to get it to hell over with, what do you think?"

Ray said, "Son send your girlfriend to town, there may be fireworks out here and she might get hurt."

Jenean didn't question him, she just grabbed what she needed, kissed him goodbye, then hugged her father and was gone.

The two men grabbed rope, a water jug and hammer and nails then began the climb up to the grave site. When they arrived old Boomer came out from the brush wagging his tail. Darran had never seen a filthier dog in his life. Boomer looked more dead than alive and smelled like it too. Both men dodged Boomer and went about lowering the box come casket into the hole. When they got it there things began to happen. First Boomer began whimpering and his hair rose up. Darran grabbed the sword and gently placed it at the bottom of the casket. Ray and Darran retreated back down the hill a bit and let things take their course. Boomer stood at the edge of the grave growling and twitching all over. Suddenly there was a loud swishing noise and the ground began shaking all around the grave site. Boomer let go a howl that was his normal howl and was knocked to the ground six feet away from the hole. Darran and Ray were scared half to death but Darran knew it was time. He ran to the hole and threw the lid on the box and started hammering sixteen penny nails in to fasten it down.

There was noise coming from inside the box that really petrified him. A muffled scream literally scared the piss out of him; he could feel it running down his leg. Still he continued hammering nails in the lid. Ray was shaking all over and feared he would wet his pants too. Boomer was rolling all over the place and only stopped when the last nail was driven. He flopped on the ground and didn't move.

Ray and Darran took the shovels and worked faster than either had ever worked before. They filled the hole in in record time, piling the extra dirt up in a great mound over those ghosts grave. Neither could wait to get the hell out of there. Darran looked down at his wet pants and at Ray. He said with a begging note in his voice, "You won't tell Jenean will you Pops?"

Ray laughed and put his arm around his new friend and said, "If my old prostate hadn't held back my pee, I too would have soaked my britches, so don't worry son. What you just went through back up there would make any man piss himself."

CHAPTER 20

Darran got out of bed in the dark and turned on a flashlight in order to see his way to the outhouse. His bowels had been loose for the last two days since planting those ghosts on Lonesome Mountain. He rounded the shed and stopped in surprise. There was a bright glow coming from where he and Ray had buried the ghosts. He really had a loose bowel now and knew this couldn't be a good thing. After coming out of the outhouse he ran smack into the two beautiful twin girl ghosts. They were standing there smiling at him in a friendly way. He would have crapped himself except, he had just dumped in the toilet. They were gesturing that he should follow them. He was drawn along with them without any effort on his part. They went to the back yard where the general's grave was and stopped. They pointed in unison at the general's grave with pleading eyes. Suddenly old Boomer let go with a bellow that scared Darran half to death and the twin ghosts dissipated into thin air. Darran walked on shaky legs over to the rear porch and collapsed on it. How in hell was he going to explain this to his new love?

BONDED FOR LIFE

BONDED FOR LIFE
MISSISSIPPI BOY AND GIRL

All the two did, was fall in love with each other. The rest just came naturally, they began to sneak around and see each other when they were in their early teens. By the time she was sixteen and he eighteen they had lost their virginity to each other. Neither had enjoyed the initial experience and would abstain from sex until married. They remained best friends, in spite of the messy act and by the time the boy, Tilman Bradley Ketchem, graduated from high school and went to work driving trucks for his Dad; they were looking forward to the day, when she got her diploma and then get married.

Gracy Ann Putny was a dreamer. She dreamed of moving somewhere other than Mississippi. The weather really cheesed her off at times. If it wasn't too hot it was too damn cold then it rained all the time. She and Tilman talked often of their future plans. The constant place of interest that cropped up often; was Alaska. Tilman had been interested in gold mining since he was a young pup, and hoped someday, to try it out for real. He was educated to the level of high school but had read all his life and was self-educated far above what his diploma read.

When Tilman turned twenty one, the love of his life, graduated with honors, from the Brookfield Mississippi high school, at the age of nineteen.

The two decided to get married right away. Their parents seemed to sanction the union, and held a nice wedding for the two. At the reception Tilman, with his arm around his new wife dropped his bomb shell; he and his bride would buy a camper and head out to Alaska.

Of course there was discussion both for and against the wild idea, but after seeing the calm resolve of the two determined youngsters, they sang the song, "For they are jolly good fellows, so say all of us, so say all of us."

CHAPTER 2

Tilman sometimes wondered if they had made the right decision. The Ford truck he had been driving for four years had some problems. First the thing had begun using lots of oil as soon as he put the old camper on its back in Brook town, as he called it. The truck still ran good, but left a trail of blue smoke in its wake. Tilman stopped every few miles, to put new oil in the 351 boss V-8. They were in Alberta Canada near Calgary when he pulled into a wayside to replenish the oil. After putting two quarts of 10/ 40 oil in, he asked Gracy to fire the engine up. He wanted to see things work with his own eyes. He told Gracy to race the engine. Gracy really raced the damn thing. She flat floor boarded the gas pedal, the 351 tried to jump out of its compartment. Before Tilman could get to her, he noticed the breather hose from the engine to the carburetor completely collapsed on its self. There was an embarrassing blue smoke screen all over the way side and some Canooks were looking at them strangely, Tilman finally got Gracy to lift her foot off the throttle. He knew now, why they had used up two cases of oil. The engine was choking its self to death. He simply unhooked the offending soft hose and the engine stopped using oil altogether. They ran it to the next parts store and bought a new length of hose for a few bucks, installed it, and went on their way.

In 1980, the farther they traveled north, the wilder the country became. They noticed gas and all consumer goods increased in price as well. After Edmonton Alberta, the Road turned west by north. They had traveled so long headed north; it seemed strange to be driving into the sun set each evening.

The two lovers were in no hurry, they only drove two hundred miles or so a day, and camped alongside the road or at one of the fuel stops that afforded a campsite for their customers. It was daylight almost all the time, darkness was a deep twilight.

At Dawson Creek the old Ford needed a U joint replaced. The thing had been vibrating since after Grand Prairie, and he had wished he had turned back when he noticed the rumble. By the time they pulled into Dawson Creek it was getting embarrassing to the two kids. The first place they came to was a motor repair shop that couldn't take the high camper or didn't want to.

The man grudgingly told Tilman to go to Dawson Creek propane. They work on old trucks. Tilman smiled and thanked him. He could tell the guy didn't like Americans much but he did not want any trouble with the people, he was the guest and would behave as one, although it was hard to do sometime. They found Canadian propane. They were the friendliest bunch he had found to date. They jumped on the U joint and had it done in a matter of an hour.

He found some Canadians friendly, but some were downright rude, and didn't try to hide it. A few times he stood up to them, like when he and Gracy ran out of gas a half a mile short of a remote service station. Tilman made Gracy lock the doors on the truck and with 5 gallon gas can in hand, took off hoofing it to the station. He could see it from the hill where the truck was parked. When he arrived it was open, but no one was there. Accustomed to pumping his own gas, he proceeded to do so. He turned the pump on by raising the handle and began to fill the container. All at once this Canadian was screaming at him, "What the hell do you think you're doing you American bastard?"

Tilman damn near pissed his pants. The Canadian had been hiding around the corner, laying in wait for him, He saw red. This bastard deserved a dose of his own medicine. Tilman was no small boy, He stood six foot three inches tall in his bare feet and being part Irish, he instantly became unglued. He backed the Canadian up against the next pump and pushed his chest into the smaller man's, and said `quietly; "What name did you just call me Mister?"

The butt hole turned white as a sheet and began to apologize. Tilman said, "Fill my gas jug you ass hole then I'll pay you and, I'll tell everyone I meet, about your rudeness."

Tilman was shaking and glad this was one of the exceptions and not the rule. From that time on, he let the attendant pump the gas for him.

CHAPTER 3

At Laird River, they spent the night alongside the river where a strange incident took place. After having a great cook out over one of the camp ground fire rings, they went to bed early. At three am, something woke Tilman up; He slid out of bed and was standing on the floor and didn't know why. He listened and, then opened the camper door and looked out. It was full daylight, and he saw nothing out of the ordinary. He came back to bed and snuggled up to Gracy. She mumbled in her sleep but didn't wake up. When they woke up at eight am, they had coffee and toast made in the oven. They went outside and when Tilman walked to the driver side of the truck, he yelled "HEY" so loud he scared Gracy half to death. She ran around and saw what he yelled about. The left rear wheel and tire were gone. There was an old rusty hydraulic jack holding the truck up in its place. Tilman and Gracy stood there with their mouths open. Some other campers came over to investigate. One Canadian said, "The bastards have been at it again."

Tilman, ask who the bastards might be. The_Guy said, "The Indians of course."

Tilman got the spare out from its storage place under the rear bed of the truck. He found the lug nuts on the ground, ten or so feet away. When he had the wheel and tire secured, he ask where the nearest police station was, The same, forth coming Canadian, told them it was at Upper Laird River, about one hundred miles or so north.

Tilman sure hated to drive without a spare in this country. This was the third tire they had used up on the trip so far. Now they had to have a wheel too. When they arrived at upper Laird River, they visited the Royal Mounted Police Station. The policeman on duty asked what kind of a vehicle and what color the wheels were on their truck. He told them, "Wait here I'll be right back with your wheel and tire".

This flabbergasted Tilman and Gracy. They sat down in comfortable easy chairs, and waited. Not more than twenty minutes later, the policeman was back with an Indian carrying their wheel and tire. The policeman explained; "I saw this truck parked at this young man's house yesterday with one very shredded tire. It has been there for two weeks and suddenly a tire appears out of nowhere and the truck is mobile once more. I noticed the different color rim this morning and thought something might crop up and sure enough it did, eh?"

Tilman and Gracy profusely thanked the Mountie, then Gracy, always concerned for others, ask him how much trouble the tire thief was in, he said, "That depends on you, you can drop the charges and I'll let him go, or press charges, and let him appear before the magistrate. He will probably be fined. That would be better than letting him go, don't you think EH?"

Tilman and Gracy said, "Make him pay a fine, to compensate you and the court. He needs to learn a lesson; it'll teach him to leave other people's things alone."

The Cop said, "I concur, I'll get him and take him on over and he will apologize to you, then you can be on your way."

The officer came out from the cell area with the young Indian. The fellow had a smile on his face when he said, "I'm sorry I shouldn't have taken your tire, eh, can I have my jack back?"

They all looked at the grinning Indian and couldn't believe their ears. Tilman said, "I left it there in the camp ground, sorry about that."

He was having a hard time not bursting out laughing.

The road, such as it was, stretched out forever in front of them. Sometimes they made good time but not for long. Either construction, or sharp curves and hills would crop up, and slow them down to a crawl.

The Alaskan Highway had been constructed during the Second World War as a means to transport military equipment to the war front the Japs had established; by occupying one of our western most Aleutian islands. Seems the little shits wanted to force this side of the world to learn Japanese the hard way.

In the end, all we had to do was leave the little fellows alone and the extreme temperature took care of them, in other words, they froze their asses off. After the war was over the Americans up and gave the road to the Canadians. This was akin to Greeks bearing gifts. The Canadians didn't realize they had to maintain the thing and as the country populated itself, they would have to improve sixteen hundred miles of what amounted to a goat track for four wheel drive vehicles, it's no wonder a few Canadians are peeved at United States citizens, coming up their road for free, while they have to shell out billions of bucks on it, to upgrade and maintain the thing.

Days later they arrived at Beaver Creek Yukon Territory and the Alaskan border. After they answered all the agents 'questions, Tilman then asked, "How far it was to the next gas station."

The guy looked down his nose at the couple and stated flatly, that was not his job thank you.

Tilman thought, some Canadian has rubbed off on this old boy. Tilman simply said, "Have a nice day sir" and drove across the border into Alaska. Tilman began gas saving techniques; he coasted down every hill, and took each hill as easy as possible.

A gas station hove in sight at the turn off to Northway proper, Tilman was sure he could hear a sucking sound coming from the dry gas tank.

CHAPTER 4

Tilman and Gracy had spent a ton of money on their trip up the Alcan Highway and Tilman knew they should get somewhere, where they could work. When they reached Tok Junction they turned left and lined out south for Anchorage and maybe on down to Seward on the coast.

It was exhilarating to be in love and in Alaska at the same time. The two had gotten their sex life together and couldn't get enough of each other. They would be driving down the road and look at each other and Tilman would find a place to park the camper and sometimes not the most desirable place either. One time near Glenallen he neglected to put the camper truck in park. The Ford rolled down the slight hill and nosed into the bushes where it stopped at an angle that made it hard to get out the back door. The couple was so helplessly trapped in the back of their moving truck that all thoughts of hanky panky were forgotten. Tilman jumped out in his jockey shorts and fired the truck up and backed it out of the bushes onto the black top. Gracy said, "Bet you don't do that again Huh?"

The two began laughing at the absurdity of the situation.

Anchorage Alaska is a city of mega proportions. Four thousand souls call it home and Tilman couldn't get out quick enough. It seemed to him and Gracy that all the drivers were in a hurry to get somewhere and didn't much care who they ran over to get there. Compared to Brookfield Mississippi it was a huge master mix of humanity. They drove down the Seward highway to Seward. They stayed at a rest area for the night and arrived in Seward in the early afternoon and found a neat small town that catered to tourist and had one of the premium fisheries in the State. Ice Sickle Sea Foods were hiring workers for their processing plant; according to the sign on the wall. Tilman and Gracy talked it over and made up their mind that they would give it a go.

 They would work the summer and save their money. Maybe they could find a cabin or house they could rent for the winter after they finished with this job Tilman thought maybe they would try down on the Kenai Peninsula.

 Seward fisheries hired the two on the spot and allowed them to move into quarters they would be charged for. They weren't as nice as the camper but there was a hot shower and comfortable beds. They only had to walk a short distance to the mess hall and then on to their place of work.

 They went to the mess hall and had a feed they signed for and then right after reported to be orientated and introduced to the work they would be doing.

 The two were orientated, issued rain gear, gloves and revoltingly sent to the slime line. Salmon that had been beheaded were sent down a chute to the waiting slimes. The name slime says it all. With gloved hands and a spoon tool they were shown how to remove the blood line surrounding the back bone of each fish and to de slime the disgusting thing as Gracy referred to the fish. The fish would hit three sets of hands before it was passed on to the freezer, where it was flash frozen and packed for shipment to the cannery. About half went to the Cannery right here as fresh as could be. Another line would cut the fish in steaks in a size to fit a can. The job was mind numbing and boring. Not only did the mind grow numb but so did the hands and feet. By the end of the 16 hour day Gracy swore if she had to touch one more fish she was going back home to Brookfield and never leave again. Tilman was too tired to respond in any way but to lie down and go instantly asleep. Gracy mumbled some more and then did the same. The two slept right through the night and woke up at six am and were surprised at how refreshed they felt after a quick shower. Heck maybe they could make it one more day. They dragged their tired butts over to the mess hall for breakfast and on to the slime line, repeating the messy job all over again.

_Day two at first seemed harder than the first one but after an hour they perked up and had a good time. Once they got into the rhythm of the job, time flew and it was lunch before the realized it. Tilman thought they might make it after all. He was really proud of Gracy, whom had never worked a day in her life, and was keeping up with all the rest.

_One day followed another and before they realized it, it was August and about to be all over. The two were called in to the office and offered a job out at King Salmon at their other fisheries on the west coast, but it was a fly in job and the both of them had had enough of processing fish to do them for life at least. They had plenty of money anyhow and had to find a place to live for the winter that was coming like a freight train. The boss man said he didn't blame them and they were on rehire for the next season. Neither one of them said anything in return and left the office shaking their head knowing they would never return to work here again, because they never wanted see a slim line again for the rest of their lives.

CHAPTER 5

The cabin they found was a short distance from the town of Homer and was cute as could be. It had a loft and was heated by Monitor oil stoves one in the basement and one in a living room that was as big as the cabin They were house sitting for the owners, who were down south in Phoenix. They had it until the last day of May. The cost was only three hundred a month and that, was mostly for heating oil to heat the place. The house was kinda free.

The two talked it over and agreed to go gold mining come spring. Tilman thought maybe they should take a chance and cruise the Yukon River and see if anyone had missed any gold down that way. They both agreed it sounded romantic and fun, it was a go. Tilman begin accumulating maps and any books the Library could offer him on gold mining throughout Alaska. He was pleasantly surprised to learn they mined gold right off the beach in Nome Alaska. The hot spot was the forty mile, near Eagle Alaska, but Tilman believed the early miners, due to poor mining techniques, had missed more gold then they found. He pointed Kokrines out to Gracy and they pulled all the history up the library had to offer. The town had been deserted when gold was discovered down river in Ruby back in the 1890's.

CHAPTER 6

Spring came to the North Country almost overnight. One day it was winter in Homer, and the next they could feel the heat in the sun. The snow cover shrank at an amazingly fast pace. Spring happened in Homer on the last day in May 1980. It didn't catch Tilman and Gracy by surprise. They had been ready for it as far back as March. Tilman complained to Gracy that, back home he would be duck hunting by now. She laughed at him and told him; "You are not in Mississippi now boy. You are a Chechocko here in Alaska and you better get used to it, because, this Gal ain't a gonna go back to Mississippi to live. You and I didn't spend all last summer on that disgusting slime line just to run back home."

Gracy had a fire in her eyes Tilman hadn't realized existed till now. He took her in his arms, and soothingly told her, he wasn't advocating running back, but he did miss his hunting and fishing. He said, "At the same time, I know we are in the best state in the USA for both. We just need to get out there and do it." Gracy was relaxed and hugged him back.

Fairbanks was a wild night life town of twenty five thousand people. In June no one slept, or so it seemed. Tilman and Gracy found the Norlite camp ground on Peger road and took up temporary residence with their camper. Their first day there, they found Pikes Landing. Part rollicking frontier bar, part restaurant and part Lounge, with an outdoor patio that overlooked the Chena River. The food was the best in town and not too costly. The cream of the mining community frequented the bar, both day and night. The place closed for one hour, in each twenty four hour period, from five till six am. The miners loved Gracy and were always trying to engage her in conversation. When they did, she snuggled up to Tilman and in her southern drawl introduced her husband Tilman. This always cooled their ardor and let a useful conversation take place.

Tilman was quick to stir the miner toward talking about or looking for gold. Tilman and Gracy spent most of their time out on the patio because inside one had to cut the cigarette smoke with a knife. Tilman could take the smoke better than Gracy could. She would sneeze continually when they got stuck at the bar listening to some windbag miner spout off. Sometime Tilman learned stuff but more and more they shied away from the place.

CHAPTER 7

Tilman decided on an eighteen foot freighter canoe. It had a square stern transom, to allow up to a ten horse outboard motor. Tilman chose a five horse Honda motor that used straight gas with a crank case for oil. The canoe would haul two people and up to a ton of gear. Tilman had Alaska Tent and Tarp to fabricate a cover with zip up ports, one forward for Gracy and one aft for him. They also purchased a ten by twelve foot wall tent. This was their summer lodging for Kokrines

When they were all packed up and ready to go they were given a great drunken send off, by the drinking crowd down at Pikes Landing. Tilman only drank one beer, Gracy shunned the stuff entirely. There were drunks jumping in the frigid waters of the China River, and having to be pulled out half frozen, by the not so drunk patrons.

Floating down the river out of hearing distance, the river emitted only a whisper and it became very peaceful. The water was a slow moving delight to the two Mississippians. Tilman got his rod and reel out and began to cast his line as they slowly drifted. He was shocked when a fish hit his lure with a mighty blow. The thing stood on its tail and danced as long as a minute, then dove to the bottom of the river. Tilman had set his drag and it slowed the fish somewhat and took a lot of work for it to reach its goal. The thing broke water one more time, then Tilman was able to pull it to the canoe and land it. Gracy looked in her little book and exclaimed excitedly, it was a Dolly Varden, an excellent fish to eat.

Tilbert cleaned the fish, and began to look for a place to prepare a meal. Before he could find one, the Chena dumped into the Tananna River. This river was Glacier fed, and was loaded with silt. It was a dirty muddy brown fast moving hunk of water. Gracy took one look and told Tilman they should go back. Tilman half agreed with his lovely wife and fired the motor up and turned up stream. They ran about half a mile, found a camp site and set up the wall tent, then made a fire. The mosquitoes were almost as bad as on the bayou down in Mississippi.

After a feed, the two talked things over and agreed the River would more than likely clear up where it met the Yukon, coming out of Canada, down near The Village of Tananna. Tilman fished all afternoon, and landed six good sized Dollis. He dressed each one and after salting them down good, hung them in the sun to dry. They would have meat for the trip down the muddy Tananna.

Tilman didn't know it, but the muddy water did not affect fishing one bit. But it made for a happier Gracy, so it was worth it. They both had a lot to learn about living in this manner. Tilman was happy his beautiful bride was willing to give it a shot and not give up on going down river. They had put the camper in storage in Fairbanks, and paid a year advanced rent. They should know by then, if they could make a living mining gold in Alaska.

CHAPTER 8

Tilman knew he had made a mistake. This slough was a dead end. The Yukon had fallen six or seven feet since break up. The winter ice and snow melt off, had flooded the Yukon, then went away and left this slough with a high and dry spot where a small creek entered. He gently beached the canoe and they got out on shore, the dead end slough was in a nice area. Tilman grabbed his gold pan, as he had done at each creek since Tananna and headed towards the creek with Gracy tagging along behind him. He squatted down at the stream and rinsed his gold pan out and tasted the water, it was sweet, and it flowed through black sand. Tilman dipped a pan full of sand and small rock and swirled it around and around letting the sand and rock leave the pan in a controlled amount. When down to real small stuff, he poked through it, and let out a yell that scared the bejebbers out of Gracy. He said, "Look at this honey."

He showed her color in the bottom of the pan, then dipped more water and washed the rest of the sand and pebbles out and there it was, Gold! Tilman couldn't believe their luck. If not for a dead end slough, they would have passed it right by. Tilman put the gold in a vial and did another pan. It came up looking as rich or richer than the first one did. His heart was going a mile a minute. This was one of the missed creeks, all because of the dead end slough.

He guessed back when it had been common knowledge among the miners this was a dead end, and for the most part every one dodged it. Tilman noticed where he found gold; it was down to bed rock. He needed to stake his claim the moment they arrived back in Fairbanks. But this summer he and Gracy would see how much gold they could retrieve from this hidden creek. They took a hike up the overgrown creek and found a beautiful flat mossy infested camping site, they had brought six cans of Off bug spray with them, and thank god they did. They were so thick; one had to wear head gear to keep from breathing them in

After setting up camp and clearing out all the brush and burning it in little fires all around the camp sight. The mosquito population decreased considerably. Tilman decided to teach Gracy how to shoot his Stevens twelve gauge pump shotgun. He had broken her in on the three fifty seven long barrel Colt and she did pretty well with it. She could hit things he pointed out on the bank as they floated down river.

The shotgun was a different sort of animal. For one thing, it kicked hard and could knock a small gal like Gracy on her butt, and for another, the only ammo Tilman brought with them, was one ounce lead slugs and buck shot.

The gun had a modified choke so as not to split the barrel when fired. Tilman showed Gracy how to become a part of the gun. He had her practice sucking the gun to her body and dry firing the piece. When she looked good, he loaded it with a round.

When she sucked the gun in and squeezed the shot off, she was rocked back, but caught herself and bounced back. Gracy was grinning so broadly, it made her light up like a jack-o-lantern. She sat the gun down and hugged Tilman. She said, "Can I shoot it again"? Tilman said, "Ok but let's make a situation for this one. Turn your back Hon. and I'll put a make believe bear for you to shoot at."

Whatever is out of place, when you turn around is a charging bear. You must shoot him right in the face. Tilman ran back to the canoe and grabbed one of the boxes they had unpacked goods from. He ran back, and yelled as he ran, don't peek Hon.

He set the box down, and then moved back behind the tent. He Yelled, "Bear!"

Gracy turned and fired, she blew that box all to hell and gone. She was real excited now. She exclaimed, "Bad ole bear better not come around here."

Gracy blow his ass off. Tilman got so tickled he rolled on the ground and almost peed himself. He sure had a funny wife. She piled on top of him and then it turned serious, and they stopped laughing!

CHAPTER 9

Ooh, that feels soooo good. Gracy Ketchem was buff naked sitting in the steaming water of a geothermal hot springs near the defunct village of Kockrines Alaska. The water was scalding on one side and icy on the other. The trick was to mix the two with body movements. This was the best bath they'd had since coming down from Fairbanks in their canoe, and finding gold in a remote creek that flowed into the Yukon River.

They had worked their backsides off all summer in this creek, and had extracted 7 vials of gold and a double hand full of nuggets that ranged from pea size up to the largest, the size of a golf ball that should bring a good sum of money at the Fairbanks Gold Exchange.

They had to work harder and longer the farther they progressed up the creek because of increased overburden. They had to remove all that to get down to bed rock where the gold collected. The little two inch dredge, then would pick up any gold and run it along with sand and rock through the metal ripples, where the gold remained behind while the sand and rocks, being lighter, went on through. The first time they found a bunch of nuggets at cleanup was an exciting time for the two miners. Gracy and Tilman were hooked forever, and would look for gold for the rest of their lives.

The Yukon rose after rains up stream in its collection basin, and Tilman and Gracy had to move their camp up the creek. The water was twenty feet away when they made their move.

The new camp was not as nice as the old one, but Tilman cut underbrush down all around the wall tent, and made it livable. Their gold was under water, so they took a few days off and went exploring up in the hills above Kockrines. On their second day they got a great surprise. They literally ran into two old trappers with backpacks on that looked far too heavy for them to carry. The old men were ready for a break and shucked their packs on to the ground and set down on them. Introductions were made then. Their names were Shane and Joseph. They were the only fulltime occupants of Kockrines, and fished in the summer time and trapped during the winter. They were a crusty two, and took a shine to Gracy, who was the first female the two old men had seen in two years, other than Indian ladies that were mostly old and dried up. Shane spoke up and said, "Ye be a fine lass me young girrl. If I be a few yeers yonger, I be after ye like some starven Mon."

His Scottish brogue became more pronounced as he spoke. They all laughed, and Tilman knew he would grow to like this old Scotsman. Joseph was a quite one and only spoke if spoken to. Gracy tried to draw him in to a conversation, but it was short lived. He asked Tilman, "What you do on Yukon?"

He was blunt in his speech and caused the two young folks to withdraw a bit from their normal openness. Tilman answered with, "Looking for gold."

Joseph asked "Find any?"

Tilman said, "If I did, that would be my business, don't you think."

Joseph grinned at them and said, "You told me eh? You right, none of my business, but I think you find gold and I say good for you. Go to Fairbanks and register claim. We protect your gold while you gone."

Tilman thought this Indian was smart, and began to warm up to him.

The two old men were the ones to tell them about these hot springs they were enjoying so much right now. They had visited them a couple of times and had dinners consisting of moose and fish with garden vegetables. The two sourdoughs were the best entertainers Gracy and Tilman found out here, and were a dictionary for Yukon lore. Shane came here after the big war in the fortys. He had jumped ship in Anchorage Alaska, then made his way out here and swore he would never go back.

He had been in trouble on the ship. A merchant marine vessel out of Glasgow Scotland. He was a cook and worked for one of the meanest men he had ever known, the bugger would steal stores and sell them on the black market at each port they visited, then blame it on Shane. Young Shane was called before the skipper where he declared his innocence. The Capitan told him he would be brought up on charges when the boat returned to Glasgow. In the mean time he would receive only 10% pay until the charges were answered. Shane left the ship that night by swimming in the cold North Pacific Ocean for a hundred feet and climbing up on a sail boat that was sistered to other boats. He was near dead when the owner came top side to see what had boarded his craft, and discovered him huddled on the poop deck shaking so bad he couldn't be stilled.

The skipper hustled him below where a diesel stove warmed him up in a few minutes. The skipper wanted to know where he had come from. As soon as he could Shane explained what happened. The skipper said, "That dirty devil of a skipper had no business taking your money until you were proven guilty. I don't blame you for not sticking it out. What do you intend to do now?"

Shane said, "I'm open for suggestions, do you have any?"

The skipper, Bernie, liked this foreigner and told him the truth. This place Alaska isn't a state yet, but it is a territory, and must have immigration laws. I think you should disappear into the interior, get lost, and don't worry about it. If you want, you can stay aboard for my trip around to Valdez, it's pretty close to the interior from there; you can make your way out on the Yukon River system and start a new life.

Joseph's story wasn't quite so colorful. He had been born in Galena, a couple hundred miles downriver. He was Athabasca Indian and Irish. He had a strange sense of humor, and kept them in stitches most of the time. He had a woman down in Galena that he called mean old bitch as often as he could. He said, "She stay there and I stay here, and if I see her coming, I hide in hills."

Tilman and Gracy made love on the rocks beside the hot spring. They kept an ear open for airplanes, but weren't interrupted during their time together. They bathed once more, and then dressed for the return trip to the camp in the canoe. As they approached their gravel bar in the slough they saw another boat there and two seedy looking men walking around on their claim. Tilman handed the shotgun to Gracy and exchanged a look with her. He loosened his 357 and flipped the hammer safety strap off its snap. He said, "Howdy folks, can we help you with anything?"

His greeting was met with silence and blood shot eyes. He said. "I've ask you nice once now, what do you want in our camp."

The tallest one spoke then, "I don't think you own this creek buddy, and we are looking around and there's not much you and that hotty totty there with you can do about it."

This set Gracy off like a cheap firecracker. She stepped off the canoe on to the gravel with the shotgun leveled at the one who had done the talking. She said, "I may well be hotty totty, but let's not make any mistake here shit head. This old gun is loaded with steel ball bearings and I have you both in my sights and I kill bears all the time with it."

Tilman pulled his pistol out and said, "And if she misses I won't.Get in your boat and hit the River NOW!"

The two almost broke their necks getting in their boat and getting it started. They tore out down River leaving two shaking kids in their wake. Tilman and Gracy set down on the rock, Tilman said, "Boy that was close" Then he calmly asked, "Just when did you shoot all those bears sweetheart?"

They talked it over and decided it would be best to go up river and file a claim on this creek. They went to talk to Shane and Joseph about the two men they had run off. Shane become excited and said, "I know those two, they are bad news. They come from Ruby Alaska 120 miles downriver. This used to be their town back when gold was mined here." He settled down and Tilman and Gracy knew they were in for a whale of a story.

Shane began by telling them how someone had taken a crap on the alter of the one Catholic Church in town. The priest was incensed to the point that he called a meeting of the entire population and by damn everyone had better be there. The priest tried to find out who the culprits were but it was not to be. No one came forward to admit guilt. This really pissed the good Father off and he there and then declared grass would grow over all the streets starting now. Well the miners and Indians stopped walking on the streets and low and behold grass began to grow in them. Then gold was discovered down at Ruby creek where the town by that name exists today. Every person in Kockrines moved in mass to Ruby. The town of Kockrines would be totally uninhabited for the next 50 years, until a Scotsman by the name of Shane arrived on a log raft.

In mid-August the Yukon became clear enough to drink from, and the nights become cold and a frost would be on everything come morning. Tilman and Gracy said goodbye to Joseph and Shane and pointed their canoe up river. The little canoe sliced through the water at thirty-five mph with a much lighter load then the down River trip. Their gear was stored with the old sourdough's at Kockrines. They had been warned about gravel bars that would rip the bottom end out of their little Honda engine, and how to avoid them. Tilman found if he kept an eye on the shore line he could see the gravel bar coming out of the water and turning into a ridge on land. They stopped in the village of Tanana where the Yukon makes a left turn towards White Horse Canada. Tilman and Gracy were friendly and outgoing and soon made friends with most of the population of this thriving fishing village. They gassed up and continued on their way. The Tanana River was totally changed from when they came down in the spring. It wasn't much more than a stream and then it would split into two or three smaller streams. This made for some interesting moments. When they ran out of water, a portage would take place. If it was a long portage they simply went to the next deep water and pitched the wall tint on the shore. They could then take their time to complete the portage at leisure. Tilman and Gracy enjoyed these campouts because it gave them time together they hadn't had while working their tails off wearing calluses on their hands digging for gold. They were running short on food however and went on their way as soon as they were rested. At last they came to the mouth of the Chena River. They were near Fairbanks now and soon arrived at Pike Landing. They beached the canoe and went and had a real feed, at a table with a linen table cloth on it.

Tilman had a lot of things to take care of before they went south for the winter. He needed machinery and supplies delivered to the mine come spring. He sought out the Nenana Barge Lines representative, and asked him if the barge could stop at Kockrines to drop off a big order. The rep made a call to headquarters and smiled and said we sure can Mr. Ketchum. Whatever you buy just put this control number on it and the date to be delivered and we will do our best to get it there. We can tie up at the old landing there and lift whatever off with our crane. Our weight limit is 20.000 pounds, and that covers up to a D-4 cat. We can take bigger machines, but it will cost you much more money, because we have to carry a special ramp with us and you have to pay the freight on that.

Gracy and Tilman went to the gold exchange and filed their claim on the creek. They had the right to mine over 8 miles of that creek. When they had their gold weighed out they were staggered by the amount they had mined over the summer. They were handed a check for $320,486.22. Neither had ever seen that much money in their life. They just sat and stared at the check for a time. Finally they looked in each other's eyes and fell in each other's arms. Both knew they had been blessed by a higher power and bowed their heads and had a moment of silence. Tilman said, "Honey let's find a bank and put this thing in it."

Gracy said, "Ok honey but let's find a hotel first and have a bath".

Tilman laughed and agreed with her.

CHAPTER10

There was excitement in the cool spring air. Tilman and Gracy were on the dock of the Nenana Barge Lines at the village of Nenana, located on the Glen Highway fifty odd miles from Fairbanks. They were watching the D-4 cat being lowered to the deck of the power barge that would carry them and all the tons of gear down to Kockrines and drop it and them off. Tilman and Gracy had spent a ton of money to mine their claim, and they still had money to do whatever they had a mind to. Tilman had hired a grounder by the name of Lance Deveroux, [Dev] as he liked to be called. He had experience on cats and mining in general, and Gracy and Tilman both liked his attitude and outlook on life. Dev was older than the two youngsters but he was a worker and fell to it with exuberance. He had come to Alaska as a youngster and worked in the gold fields out around the forty mile country and around Chicken in the southeast corner of mainland Alaska. He had also driven log trucks down in southeast Alaska, but got tired of it raining buckets all the time and migrated up north to the gold fields. When Tilman and Gracy met Dev he was thinking about boating down the Yukon. When he heard of their claim, he asked if they needed any help, and the relationship developed from there. Now they were here loading up tons of gear, and would be on their way down river.

Sleeping accommodations weren't the best on the barge. One had to unroll ones sleeping bag whereever one felt he or she wouldn't be trod upon.

Even then the rumble of the big motors that was propelling the barge was a noisy lot, and made sleep impossible for the most part. Gracy was too excited to sleep anyhow. She had binoculars trained on the shoreline for hours at a time. When she saw an animal on the bank she shouted above the noisy barge, and described what it was. The crew of the barge was greatly entertained by her on going descriptions of moose, bear, porcupine and wild fowl of every type. When they passed a fish camp she would wave wildly and shout a greeting to any one on shore. Their first stop was Tannana to off load goods and pump gasoline to storage tanks. After a full day they were on their way once more.

They reached Kockrines sooner than Tilman expected, and caught him sleeping for the first time since Fairbanks. He came awake when Gracy shook him, and declared, "We are home Honey."

The offloading was about to begin by the time he was fully awake and walked down the gang plank to shore. Joseph and Shane were there and so happy to see them, they both shook Tilman's hand and hugged Gracy. Joseph Spoke up and said, "You bring good machine white man, get down to where gold hide."

Tilman introduced them to Dev and told them he would be here all summer and operate the dozer. Joseph shook Dev's hand and stated, "I see you before in Fairbanks on two street."

Dev said, "I profess my guilt, A man needs some sort of vice up here, and I'm no exception. I guess this job will cure me of that one. I've looked all

around Kockrines and don't see one flashing sign."
They all had a good laugh at that.

When the barge crew swung the D4 out onto the
beach, Tilman thought for sure the weight would tip
the barge over, but it simply grounded the barge on
the bottom and set the D4 down as gentle as a
feather. Dev was on the machine and hit the starter
button and spun it around and moved it out of the
way. Tons of gear followed and soon were stacked
next to the little dozer. Tilman and Dev took chain
saws and begin cutting spruce trees. They had to
have a sled to pull with the Cat to haul the gear up to
the mine site. Gracy went through the gear getting
things Tilman needed to build the sled. She needed
help to haul the box of 12 inch spikes to the trees
they had cut down. Dev was a hard worker and was
there before Tilman had a chance to tell him to go.
He put the heavy box on his shoulder and long
stepped to where Tilman was waiting on it. The sled
went together faster than Tilman thought it would.
Dev brought the cat over and they hooked up with a
log chain and pulled the sled over to the gear.
Joseph and Shane helped them load the tons of gear
on the 10x20 sled. Shane told Tilman they needed to
talk before they took off up river to the mine. Tilman
declared a job well done and the end of the work day
as well. They all walked to the old men's cabin. The
weather was warm for the last week in May, and they
set out side on chunks of wood robbed from the
nearby wood lot.

Shane began by saying, "There be robbers out
here me lad and lass. The two you ran off before ye

left for The City, came back after ye be gone and old Joseph here had a run in with them. The consequence of their trespass will long remain with the two would be thieves in the form of buck shot pellet scars on their arses put there by none other than me friend Joseph here. I might mention they were armed with rifles and had me at a disadvantage at the time. I think they were jumping your claim me friends, and when I confronted them they had thoughts of doing away with the two of us. Joseph had stayed back a bit, and that saved me bacon."

There was silence until Tilman cleared his throat and said, "You are on our payroll starting last fall. You did us a great service and the both of you please don't refuse what I will pay you tomorrow."

Joseph said, "I take mine now, you might die in sleep tonight." There was a huge burst of laughter from all the others.

The mining had to wait while Dev cleared a road to the mine. They could have gone up the beach but that was a dead giveaway to anyone traveling on the river that gold was being mined on their creek. Dev was an ace with the little D4. Tilman told him to not disturb the earth any more than he had to. Tilman and Gracy took their new twenty-four foot river boat up to the mine. The River was high enough they went right to the creek and to their old campsite. Thanks to their old friends nothing was disturbed that they could see anyhow. They walked up the creek for about a thousand feet or so and found a nice place to build a cabin. There was an abundance of spruce along the fringes of the creek. Tilman began falling trees and trimming them up, and then he cut them into building lengths. The mining claim rules stated the cabin had to be on skids so it could be moved.

The sled they had built to bring their gear up would, with the addition of a few more logs, do as the floor. Tilman had purchased an Adz in Fairbanks to level the round logs with. He was a bit scared of the damn thing. Just reading the warning label made his toes hurt. The thing was razor sharp and if one missed the wood and hit ones foot instead, blood would fly all over the place. Tilman thought to himself, I wonder if we could get used to walking on the logs like they are.

Two days later Dev hove in sight on the D4 with the sled in tow. He told them the last few hundred yards were clear and not even boggy. He had turned back and the two old guys and he had hooked up the sled and he only had to stop a time or two to re secure the load on the entire trip. Dev reckoned they were about five miles above Kockrines. The three fell to unloading and sorting the thousands of dollars of first class gear. Just after they got started Joseph and Shane came up the trail from the river. Tilman noticed they weren't even breathing hard. These two were in excellent health. With five sets of hands they were soon down to the floor of the sled, and had six piles of gear on plastic to be stored as they completed a storage place. Joseph said, "Build cache first, keep bears out of food."

Tilman said, "OK Joe, Take Dev and make a cache up in one of those trees."

Dev fell right in with Joe and the two had a working food storage cache at the end of the day.

Tilman had surprised himself and by that evening one could walk across the floor without stubbing their toe. Shane and Gracy spent the day peeling the bark off the logs Tilman had cut three days ago. The two worked well together and had the job finished in early afternoon.

The weather warmed as the days passed, and the cabin took form and started to resemble a building Tilman could be proud of. A lean-to was being constructed on each side of the 16x20 cabin, and the sled could be pulled away when moving day arrived. Gracy told Tilman the river was going down and he and she went down to look at it. The gravel bar was just starting to expose its self and they probably would be able to start dozing a little above where they had left off last fall, then come back later on and do the part they would miss. Tilman went in search of Dev, finding him hard at work chinking logs with pink insulation. He was gone like shot and had an upper body wash in the ice cold creek. Then he mounted the cat and began removing the overburden where Tilman indicated. There was only three feet of rock and dirt and the cat made short work of it. Tilman couldn't help but think of how he and Gracy had labored last summer to do only a fraction of what the cat did in a few minutes. It would always make them respect money however, and that was a good thing he reckoned.

The new four inch dredge had a phenomenal suction that went deep and pulled more stuff from the cracks then the two inch would ever do. The first clean up was a shocker. There was more gold then they had taken all last summer. Tilman shouted, "Everyone just got one hell of a raise."

A shout went up from all hands and Gracy. Tilman sat down in a daze. He realized he had hit the mother lode. He also realized they would have to re-mine what they had mined last year. The new dredge was worth every penny he and Gracy had paid for it. He called a meeting and when all were assembled he said. "I want you all to know we really appreciate your friendship and your hard work. What I'm about to hook you three up with should please you. As of now we are employee owned. After paying the gear off you will receive a share of the profits equal to mine and Gracie's share. There will be a 40% retention of money for future prospecting other deposits. The rest will be divided equally among us and I will be the CEO and Gracy the finance secretary. We need more people and Gracy and I will go to Fairbanks for a few days, and look for some, so let's mine while the sun shines and you guys learn how to do everything except run the cat. We don't want to have break downs, and Dev is a pretty good operator. If you want to know how much you made today, see me later after we weigh this mess."

Tilman set down on a stick of wood and took his hat off. He said, "My god honey we're rich do you know that?"

There is more than twice the amount of gold here than what we cashed in last fall. He had to tell the men, but the old guys had already taken off for their home in their boat. Dev was fast asleep in the north lean-to. The two Mississippiens were too excited to sleep so they took a walk down to their boat. The mossies were thick so they wore their head nets, and sprayed deep woods on themselves. Tilman said, "Honey we are some kind of lucky; we not only have a great gold claim, but have found some good friends and workers as well. I believe God has truly blessed us and I think we should consider starting a family soon."

Gracy said, "Honey there's no time like the present." as she snuggled up to Tilman. The boat was about to be initiated.

CLOSE CALL

CLOSE CALL
CHAPTER 1

As Clyde Brown topped over the hill and tapped his foot brake, it fell to the floor and he realized he had just been handed a bucket full of the smelly stuff in his life. There were no brakes on this piece of junk and he was in for a real hairy trip down Turkey Mountain.

There was three miles of eight percent grade; he had no choice but to navigate down this mountain using his engine as his only brake. The vehicle Clyde found himself driving on that fateful day was an old Studebaker pickup that defied description. The truck belonged to his brother anyhow and his brother didn't exactly play with a full brick. He had agreed to help him out, by driving this piece of junk down to Jenks for him and right now he couldn't think of one good reason not to kick the crap out of him; that is if he got off this mountain with his life still intact.

He tried shifting down, but that was about like trying to reinsert tooth paste back in the tube. Each gear he put the old Studebaker in seemed to cause the piece of crap to go faster. Then something came loose underneath with a great slapping noise and he was in freewheel mode now for sure. The truck made a great buck in the air as the drive shaft, that had fallen down, dug into the gravel road. It hoisted the truck high in the air in the back end. This almost caused Clyde to do two things; he came near filling his fruit of the looms and damn near had a heart attack at the same time. At a thundering speed of sixty miles per hour, all Clyde could do now, was ride er out.

What bothered our scared Clyde the most was, he knew there was a four way stop at the bottom of this three mile grade and if his calculations were anywhere near correct, he might be doing about a hundred and fifty miles per hour when he came to that four way stop sign.

Clyde smoked a pipe and had it in his mouth now. The closer the four way stop sign came, the harder he bit down on the stem of that pipe. He was breathing hard and the little spark in the bowl had come alive and there was a full stream of smoke coming from the now glowing pipe.

As the Studebaker screamed ever faster towards the crossing, Clyde had his life flash before his eyes.

He was an old Oklahoma Boy and had grown up near Jenks out on the Arkansas River. He had spent his early years roaming the sand hills of Oklahoma while hunting squirrel and rabbit. The family ate the things he and his one brother killed. Clyde didn't take any pleasure in killing, but Arvel did. He'd rather shoot something than to eat. If Arvel couldn't shoot something to eat, then he would resort to shooting stray dogs and cats. This caused Clyde to kick his younger brother's butt when they were in their pre-teens. Clyde told him if he caught him shooting puppies or neighbors cats again, he would kick his ass good. Arvel worshipped his older brother and to Clyde's knowledge, Arvel refrained from killing anything he couldn't eat after that.

Clyde remembered how his brother Arvel couldn't handle a regular job, because he just didn't have the smarts. He took care of Arvel as well as he could, but he couldn't dodge the draft for Korea. They came for him with the threat, that if he didn't go to this police action, he would in fact go to jail. When he tried to explain that his brother had no one but him, it fell on deaf ears. The draft board simply gave his brother a draft notice too. The day they reported for induction in Tulsa, Arvel was flat refused entry into the hall, where they were to be sworn in. After Clyde had raised his hand and repeated all those words, he was told to go that way please, but Clyde simply disobeyed his first order and went to his brother. He found Arvel sitting on the concrete, beside the walk outside. He had croc tears rolling down his cheeks. It near broke Clyde's heart and he really didn't know what to do. Arvel said. "Brother, they said I wasn't old enough to be in the Army."

He grabbed his brother by the shoulder and drug him back inside. He looked around for someone of authority. He saw a man in uniform with tracks on his shoulders and pulled his brother right over to him. The Captain was shocked by the sight of these two country bumpkins coming at him like a freight train. Military curtsy hadn't been taught Clyde, so he blundered right in, catching the Captain completely off guard. Clyde shouted so loud at the man, that the officer cringed. He said, "You look at what you are trying to do. My brother cannot be left alone in this world, just because you need cannon fodder in a far off land."

Clyde run down then and set down in a chair, pulling Arvel down with him. The Captain regained his equilibrium and composure. He finally sat down opposite the two and said, "Maybe we can do something about your situation son. Tell me what you and your brother's names and addresses are."

He wrote them down and then asked, "Where are your parents son?" Clyde remembered how he told that officer about his parent's death.

CHAPTER 2

It was getting close to the time for Clyde to put both hands over his eyes and give his heart to God, then kiss his ass goodbye, but the careening pickup would for sure roll over and over then, and kill him dead as a door knob anyway. He had both hands on the steering wheel clamped down so hard that they hurt. He thought back to that day when the Army Captain told them he would try to help them.

He explained to the officer that his mother had come down with consumption or something and just wasted away, until one morning she was dead. Their father had drunk some all their life, but now he really got serious about it. He got so mean; that the two boys spent most of their time camped out on the river. When they did come home, there would be much hell raising at them, making them want to go away once more. The father had a bunch of Indian in him and it really came out when he got drunk. A few times he tried to beat the boys into submission, but Clyde was smart enough to prevent real damage to themselves. He would take his brother out of the house each day before the old man woke up. They become woodsmen in this manner and always had enough to eat. Clyde worked some when he could down at the lumber yard. He unloaded ninety pound sacks of cement off a rail car for a buck an hour. He tried to get the owner to hire Arvel, but when the owner talked to his brother, it went nowhere, and really pissed Clyde off, enough that he eventually up and quit. The boys simply grew a good garden, on the five acres of river bottom and killed deer, rabbits, and squirrel for meat.

They came home one day and found the old man dead. He had drunk too much and killed himself. The boys just buried him beside their mother, and went on with life. There was nothing they knew to do about them becoming orphans, but Clyde was seventeen and Arvel was fifteen. Clyde felt they could make it on their own. That was, until Clyde turned eighteen and got his butt drafted into the Army.

Clyde saw a car pull up and stop at the four way stop and turn his way. He passed that car doing a hundred at least. The Studebaker almost sucked the other car off the road. Clyde looked in his rear view mirror and the car wound up on his side of the road after they passed each other. He was only about a quarter of a mile from being smashed to bits and clamped too hard on his pipe and bit the stem completely into two pieces. The fire bowl fell into his lap and the ball of fire fell out and rolled down in between his thighs. He was faced with a choice, either have scorched balls or let the damn pickup go its own way. When smoke began rising up from between his thigh's, from his now burning blue jeans, he scrunched up the back of the Studebakers worn out seat back and with his right hand he attempted to put the fire out that was burning his privates. The pickup was moving from one side of the road to the other.

Vernon Johnson came to the four way stop sign from the north. He normally never even tried to stop at this unnecessary stop sign. His reasoning was, that a half blind man could see for a mile in all directions and the stop sign was just something those som a bitches up in Tulsa, had installed to make trouble. However, on this day, when he looked left he got the shock of his life. There, careening down the road from left to right and back was a green Studebaker pickup, going faster than the law would ever allow. Vernon got all over his brakes and pissed his pants at the same time. Things were falling off that pickup and Vernon knew damn well he wasn't going to be able to stop in time, because he was doing at least thirty miles per hour, like he always did when going to town. The old Chevy ton and a half Vernon was driving just seemed to go faster as he approached the stop sign. Vernon took his foot off the brake and floor boarded the tired two hundred ninety two cubic inch six cylinder engine. The two trucks were on a path of destruction for sure. The only thing that saved Vernon and Clyde's life that day was the huge difference of the two vehicles speed. If the engine in the ton and a half had been less tired, both men would have died. When Vernon floor boarded the old engine however, the truck stayed at thirty miles per hour. The Studebaker was doing somewhere over a hundred miles per hour and when Vernon reached the stop sign, the Studebaker went across the front end of the Chevy, so close that Vernon lost control of the truck and wound up in the field across the road. He smelled something awful and realized he had filled his shorts. Clyde was in no better shape, he too had filled his shorts and still had to contend with a Studebaker that wasn't slowing down much, but he did put the fire out when he pissed all over himself. The levy hill slowed him a small amount and when he looked down he glanced at the speedometer, it read eighty-five. The only hope he had now, was five mile hill and that would present another problem. When he stopped on that hill going up, he still had to come down. In his present state, Clyde didn't much want to be a public spectacle, but if he jumped out of the thing when he slowed down, he would be. When his speed was near thirty miles per hour, he simply put the heap of crap into the right hand ditch. The Studebaker ground to a stop, just before a culvert and when Clyde tried to remove his clamped fingers from the wheel he couldn't at first. Finally one by one they came loose, but hurt like thunder. Now here he was his pants full of crap and a wet burnt ass. People were gathering around Vernon's old Chevy truck, but when they smelled crap they backed off real fast. The same happened when the Oklahoma highway patrol approached the Studebaker. The Trooper got one whiff of Clyde and backed off thirty feet. He asked Clyde if he was alright and Clyde said, "Hell no, do I look or smell alright?"

The officer had a hard time keeping a straight face. He finally got his emotions under control and said. "Sir, you failed to stop at that stop sign back there and almost hit that Chevy truck, do you know that?"

Clyde just set there in astonishment. Then he realized this officer didn't know the full story yet. He began explaining what happened and soon the Trooper got a sympathetic look on his face and said, "I'll call an ambulance to come and get you sir."

Clyde thought, since I have burnt my balls so severely, that wasn't such a bad idea.

While waiting on the ambulance, Clyde recalled the findings of the draft board concerning his induction into the Army. They had discharged him on a hardship discharge and he had helped his brother start a junk business and that's how come he had been driving this dilapidated old Studebaker. He was doing his brother a good turn, while his brother drove his newer truck home. Clyde had taken the Turkey mountain road home; because, there wasn't likely to be any law about, out on the dirt road. Never again he thought, but he did love his brother and never is a long time.

CRASHED IN THE ROCKIES

CRASHED IN THE ROCKIES
CHAPTER I

Denver International Airport fell behind, as he put the Cessna one-eighty-two, into a five hundred feet per minute climb, at a heading of two-hundred-seventy-five degrees, west over and through the rocky mountains, on his way to Reno Nevada to visit his kids. He was Randy McNolty, and he was an oil man from down in west Texas, near Odessa. He had left Odessa Airport the day before, after saying good bye to his new wife of two years. He had tried to convince Joden he wanted her with him, but she was a pretty clueie old gal, and knew deep down her husband needed this time alone with his two kids. They would go camping for two weeks, and talk about old times, old times that she felt she might have had a part in destroying for Randy. She went home to Mississippi for the two weeks.

He leveled off at ten thousand feet, and leaned the little opposed engine out. He passed over the rim of the Rocky Mountains, and began to drop down in altitude. The Mountain peaks were so near he felt he could reach out and touch them.

Randy glanced at the cylinder head temperature and noted it was a bit high. He pushed the mixture control forward and the needle moved down, into the normal range. A few minutes later he noticed it had climbed up once again. He put the mix control full forward and waited for the temp to drop, but it didn't. He ran down through the Instruments. The oil pressure was reading a little low; this was likely because of the high cylinder head temperature. Just as Rick reached for the throttle, the oil pressure fell to zero. He chopped the throttle and looked below him. All he saw was mountains. He had just crossed the great back bone of the Rockies, and there weren't even any towns in sight. He keyed his microphone and called a mayday, but there was no response on the radio. This didn't surprise Randy. He was behind a mountain range, and it was a long way to civilization west of here. His flight plan called for VFR to Rollins radio in Wyoming, and direct to Reno. He made up his mind to land somewhere that wouldn't kill or worse yet leaves him incapacitated so that he had to die a slow horrible death. The little opposed engine began to shake and vibrate. He turned the Master off and pulled the mix control fully to the rear. The prop continued rotating until he pulled the nose up and then it stopped wind milling. He saw a break in one of the valleys to his right, and tipped his wing over and lined up on it. He checked his glide and thought he would make the trip in the mountain. His options were, he could jump with his chute or land the damn thing. If he jumped he would be at the mercy of the elements with nothing but a parachute for survival in a wilderness so dense that he might not see another human for days or weeks. If he landed and survived the resulting crash however he might save some of the many goodies he had packed in his baggage compartment of the plane before he left Odessa.

His two children were living with his ex-wife out in Reno were true blue McNolty. Tawny, his daughter, was ten going on twenty-one. The divorce has been particularly difficult for her. She loved both her father and mother, and couldn't understand why she had to go through life without either one of them being available for her all the time. His son Jepson was a complete opposite; he wanted to be with his Dad and didn't give a sniff about his mother, or her stiff upper lip husband. At eight years old, he was making plans to convince his Dad to take him away from this total idiot, his mother had married, or he would take himself away. He was glad she had done it while he and Tawny were off camping with their Father, at least they didn't have to suffer through that wedding. Rick had shopped long and hard for all the goods in the plane. He had two boxes of candy bars, one Butterfinger and one Milky Way. He had found these two huge fruit cakes, and bought them for the two kids. His ex-wife hated the things, and that made it worthwhile, because his kids loved them. He also had his survival kit in the plane, and couldn't fathom surviving in the wilderness without it. There were emergency rations that would sustain one person two weeks, so added together he was good for at least a month.

After reasoning all that out, Rick decided to crash land. He was at five thousand feet altitude, but only eight hundred feet above the forest. He sat the little plane up as well as he could, said a prayer, thought of his new wife and his two kids, and nosed the craft towards what looked like pressure ridges left by a receding glacier. He knew it was going to be rough. As he flared out and picked a ridge ahead for his gear to hit, he pulled the wheel all the way back in his gut. He watched the air speed bleed off till the stall warning buzzer sounded out and then the gear hit the ridge and folded like match sticks. He glanced at two holes that appeared at his feet where the gear had been attached. He looked at where he was going, and saw another ridge coming at him through the wind screen. The plane had lost much of its speed when it hit the ridge that removed the gear. It slammed prop first into the next ridge. He saw sand and gravel hitting the wind shield. He ducked his head, but the window held, even covered with sand and gravel. He popped his shoulder harness and opened the cabin door. He stumbled over large rocks getting away from the plane; he made it to the baggage compartment, and popped the handle and began ripping things out of it. He laid everything far enough away, that if it burned he would still have survival gear. He then looked the plane over. There was no sign of fire, so he opened the battery compartment and unscrewed the battery quick release. There was fuel dripping from the left wing tank. He looked at it and decided to let it drain, because, he had ran most of the fuel out of that tank getting here from Denver. The other tank seemed ok. He considered himself a lucky man. Most crashes ended in fire and injuries or death. He began putting his gear back in the large baggage compartment. He was also fortunate in the fact that he had shelter, something most crashes never afforded. The cabin was mostly intact, with the exception of two gaping holes where the gear had been attached. He took two life saver cushions and stuffed them in the holes. The cabin would be warmer than the outdoors although a bit cramped. Rick checked his Emergency Locater transmitter box to make sure it was working. His heart fell; the red blinking light was out, it always blinked each time he looked at it before. He had it serviced just before he left on this trip. There was no reason it shouldn't be sending out a constant beep. He tapped it and it stayed dead. His chances of rescue went down the scale somewhat with this discovery. His not making radio contact with green river would set in motion a rescue mission looking for a proverbial needle in the hay stack.

CHAPTER 2

John Shakelton set in thought about what he should do. He was a member of the Salt Lake City Civil Air Patrol. He had just received a call from the FAA at Rawlins Wyoming that a small plane was missing between Denver and Salt Lake. He knew that country, and this wasn't a gonna be a picnic, he thought. John had spent twenty years in the US Army, thirteen of it as an aviator, and seven as a mechanic. When he retired, he wasn't through flying, so he bought himself a tail dragger J-3 Piper cub, slung an extra fuel tank under the belly and joined the civil air patrol. He was now the wing leader, with an office and a paycheck each week. He was living pretty well, and was thinking about up grading to a better aircraft, but sometimes he wondered if a better one existed.

The Cub was slow but, completely reliable and easy to maintain. It was also easy on gas. With the thirty gallon extra tank, he had forty-two gallons of AV gas, and could remain in the air for eighteen hours if he leaned her out well.

John went out into the hanger to talk to his friend and second in command Fuzzy Belton, about the missing plane. Fuzzy was up to his elbows on a de-Havilland R-985 Beaver engine. He was mumbling to himself something about, this dad burned Canadian piece of junk and its fuel pump location anyhow. John stood and listened to Fuzzy for a minute, Fuzzy had no idea he was there. He mumbled to himself, I'll fix you dad-gum thing, when I get this new fuel pump installed, on test flight I'm a gonna fix your Canadian butt. I'll fly you straight to the Canadian border and bail out and let you go home on your own, you, you, you . . .   John was silently laughing so hard he thought he might just pee his pants, when Fuzzy stood up on the maintenance platform to stretch the kinks out, he noticed his friend standing there below on the floor, doubled over with mirth. He grew red in the face and blustered, "What the hay do you think you're doing sneaking up on a fellow like that?"

He immediately began to laugh along with his friend. John said, "Let me know when I should say farewell to the old beaver, Pal." This made the two friends crack up with laughter once more.

John told Fuzzy about the lost aircraft and the request from the FFA for search assistance, and would he mind taking the helm while he took the cub out and looked for the wreck. Fuzzy said, "Not a problem boss, I've got more to do to this hunk of junk than ever. I need a new air plane, that's all there is to that. John told Fuzzy to call in all other pilots that were available for search and fill them in on the details. He ran off some copy's for the new pilots, then kicked the tire and lit the fire, took off and circled the field until he had enough altitude to clear the mountains east of Salt Lake, then turned north east, and at the thundering speed of eighty knots mounted the search for Rick McNolty downed airplane.

CHAPTER 3
Day one

Rick began noticing his surroundings, after getting over the mild shock of his lucky landing. Those ridges were six foot deep gouges, put there with great pressure by the movement of the Glacier, when it was here. He climbed the ridge he hit with the nose of the aircraft. He could look around and see that he was a quarter of a mile from the stream that descended from the snow line at a steep angle. That would be a fast moving bit of water.

He had adequate water in the survival pouch, but at some point he might have to make his way down there to replenish his supply. Rick turned and looked at his broken airplane. He had done a pretty good job of crashing the old gal. With a little major metal work she would fly again, but it was insured and she would remain right here forever. He just hoped someone spotted the wreckage and came to his rescue. He position was somewhere in the northwest corner of Colorado near the Utah and Wyoming border. This was some distance from any existing airways. He had to think the civil air patrol would find him. He took his orange parachute out of its bag and tied it to the wings. That should attract someone's attention.

CHAPTER 4
Denver civil air patrol

Adam Still house was on his way to work at the Denver International Airport, when his cell phone rang. He pulled to the side of the interstate and answered it. His buddy Jumbo Edict on said, "Hey pard, I just got off the phone talking to the FFA here in town and we've got one down that originated here at Denver. They would really appreciate a little help. There's no signal from the planes emergency locator transmitter. It was probably destroyed in the crash. They want us to find and report the location, and then they'll send a team in by helicopter to investigate."

When he broke the connection, Adam drove to the avionics hanger on the north end of Denver International, where he worked as a supervisor on the day shift. He clocked on and went to see his boss, Bad Leroy Cordell, the biggest black man he knew. Everyone liked Leroy and had nicknamed him after the song, Bad, Bad Leroy Brown. He fit the described man in the song, but was one of the nicest people Adam had ever known. He was welcomed right in. He told Leroy about the call from Edict on and the crash. Leroy said, "Take on off man; the pilot might be alive in the crash. He added the FAA will compensate the company for your pay, and maybe you will get lucky and make some points for the company. He had a grin that reached from ear to ear. Besides it's Friday anyhow. Now get, find data Boy befog da bears do."

119

They both broke out in stitches at the put on slave accent. Adam was still chuckling, when he climbed in his fully serviced by-wing converted Stinson Air Cat, and hit the starter on the 585 cubic inch radial engine. She fired and emitted a puff of smoke and then roared like the healthy engine she was. He called for and received permission to taxi to the auxiliary runway, the civil air patrol used almost exclusively. He ask ground control to file him out on a search and rescue fight plan, for west of Denver somewhere. The radio cackled, you have been so filed, go get him Air 29, stay in contact if at all possible. Call the tower on 42.5 for takeoff instructions, and have a good day Adam man."

It made him feel good he was known by first name to all the airport personnel. He had been flying out of Denver for the last six years, since leaving the service after one tour of duty in Germany, as an electronic repairman first class in the US Air force. He went to work with Denair Electronics, and had worked himself up to supervisor.

Adam learned to fly when he was in his teens, and thought about seeking a career flying in the Air force, but he just didn't feel too comfortable at the speed those Jets flew. The old Air he had put together from many different Air Cats. He found a sliding canopy, that with a few nights work he made fit. He also had a good exhaust collecting heat ring, and it kept him and his instruments from freezing up at the high altitudes he had to fly. Denver is known as the mile high City, and the moment you lifted off, you ascended to colder weather.

Adam heard a voice in his helmet. It was his buddy Jumbo Edict on in his J-3 cub search plane. He said, "Slow down a bit buddy, so I can catch you".

He keyed his microphone and Said, "OK Pal you got it".

Rick reached up and pulled the throttle back to seventeen hundred RPM slowing the Cat down to seventy-four knots. He dropped his flaps fifteen degrees and that brought the plane down to fifty-seven knots and five hundred feet per minute climb at 275 degrees. Rick was trying to follow the path of the downed aircraft. Flying this slowly, he had plenty of time to look around down below. All he saw was green, and greener. The wreck should stick out like someone waving a flag. Even if it hadn't burned. He looked over at his wingman and waved, then brought his flaps to zero and hit his throttle. The Cat and the Cub flew mostly at the same speed of eighty-five knots. Their speed made them good search and rescue crafts. The pilot had lots of time to look for whatever he was looking for. Adam called jumbo and said, "Lets drop down for a closer look, we'll fly higher on the return trip."

Adam caught a glimpse of something not green and winged over to the right to check it out, he realized he was looking at a glacier bed, and winged back over. He said, False alarm buddy, just an old river bed. These words would come back to haunt him later.

CHAPTER 5
First Night- Second Day

Randy McNolty was cold. The sun had disappeared like someone snuffed it out and the bitter cold came down from the mountains like a freight train express. While digging his sleeping bag out of the baggage compartment he looked at the outside air temp gauge forward of the left wing root and saw it was twenty-two degrees already and falling. He piled in to the rear seat of the one eighty two and closed the door. He unrolled his forty below mummy bag and crawled in it, shoes, clothing and all. He sat on the seat and lay down across the seat with his legs and feet on the deck. He was warm almost instantly, and was sound asleep in a minute. He woke up one time, when his nose got too cold and he pulled it inside the bag.

Randy woke up when the sun made the cabin warm and stuffy. He looked at the temperature, and saw it was seventy-nine outside. Wow what a difference he thought; probably, a seventy degree swing overnight. He checked his ration of water and found it to be quarts of ice instead of water. He made up his mind he had better sleep with the bottle from now on. He put one on the dash where sun hit it, as this was the hottest place around. He tried one of the candy bars and near broke a tooth, so he set the box where it was warm and waited for his breakfast to thaw out.

Randy hooked up the quick disconnect on his battery. When he turned the master switch on, he heard a snap of electricity, and it threw the circuit breakers, and that was that. No radio contact, his chance of rescue went down the scale again. He would have to get lucky now. Someone would have to fly right over the crash site in order to see him.

CHAPTER 6

John Shackelton flew in the general direction of Denver. He would cross paths with the estimated route the downed aircraft could have taken. There were a bunch of variables involved, the pilot may have just gone off course, had a heart attack or any one of a dozen more things that could pop up. No one could tell. He had his emergency monitor on in case the pilot still had his radio in commission. This radio also monitored the ELT that should be blasting a signal that would alert any aircraft in line with it, all the way to the Space station. There had been no report of any signal from anywhere. John surmised the ELT box was probably destroyed in the crash. He flew until he felt he had crossed the path of the downed flight, and then turned right towards Denver.

John was getting sleepy, so he brought out his thermos and poured up a large cup full. He knew he would have to use the pee horn during the flight, but cleaning it after the flight was healthier than the alternative. After the coffee, he couldn't have gone to sleep if he wanted to, and began singing at the top of his lungs. He wasn't a very good singer, but no one out here was a gonna complain, so he let- er- rip so to speak. He was just reaching a high note, when he caught his breath, and stopped singing. Off to his right was a cut in the wilderness and he thought he had caught a glimpse of color, but, It was gone in an instant. He threw the little cub in a tight right turn and increased the rpm to twenty-three hundred, and it leaped forward.

John flew to the bottom end of the rip and was flying up towards the top and "Bingo" John Shackelton's thirty years in the air, was just made all worthwhile. There standing beside his mostly intact airplane, was one lucky pilot. He had survived the crash and been found before the elements got him. John opened his window and pulled full flaps then made a low slow pass within thirty feet of the excited man. John could hear him clearly. He said, "Man I'm sure glad to see you."

John yelled, "I'll make another pass."

He went around, and came by again; he asked the pilot if he had warm clothing and food for another night. The guy shook his head yes, as John came around for the third time. He yelled, "You're a long way from any radio, I will fly back and call for an assist."

He keyed his radio and put his grasshopper forty-six call on the air. The radio cackled and a voice said, "Grasshopper forty-six this is Aig twenty-nine, a search flight of two out of Denver, over."

John said, "Aig twenty-nine your search is done. I have located the crash and have one live unhurt, I repeat- unhurt pilot in good repair. What is your position?"

Adam came back with, "Aig twenty-nine here, well, congrat's friend John, that is some great news, we are approaching the Wyoming border, how can we help?"

John said, "I'm not getting anyone on my radio, and you are closer than I am, call my position in- I'm midway up, what my jep manual describes as the

Tower Glacier, one ninety five miles on two seventy five degrees from Denver."

There was a long silence on the air. John was just about to repeat, when Jimbo said, "My buddy is beating himself up right now John, we flew right over where you are and didn't see a thing, we'll make the call and go gas up in Rawlins, and then do a fly by to check on our lucky boy."

John flew by real slow once more, and told the downed pilot, "Help is on the way, so try to keep warm until the chopper gets here."

He gave Rick thumbs up and headed for Salt Lake City. He would land after dark, on the most satisfying day of his life.

Theodore Potter

ESCAPE FROM THE SYSTEM

ESCAPE FROM THE SYSTEM

The big hawk dove at the ground with a speed that seemed much too fast, to not kill it instantly when it slammed into the ground in a plume of flying feathers. However, just before his dive ended in death, he spread his four foot wings and flared out over a mouse burrow, and extending his three inch talons, he entrapped his meal, and instantly, was airborne again with a great noisy flapping of his wings. He flew to a tall cotton wood tree where he made his home, and landed at the highest fork. The hawk held the mouse down with one talon, while he tore meat from the still alive and squealing field mouse with his beak.

The twelve year girl had watched the hawk take its meal from the safety of her hollow tree, near a branch of water that meandered down from a range of hills, that began here next to these woods, and then stretched to a high bunch of mountains called the Casans, out here in southern Tennessee. The girl wasn't far from what she knew as home. She spent most of her time out here in the woods in her hollow tree however, finding it more to her liking.

Her home life left a lot to be desired, This was because of a Father, who was drunk more often than not, and was likely to try to slip in bed with her after she was asleep. She would slip out on the other side of the bed and dive out her window. The first time he tried this, she hadn't been dressed for the outdoors and it was March, she damn near froze to death that time The only thing that saved her was the old hollow tree that had an abundance of moss and dry leaves on the floor it, where she was watching the hawk from right now.

Her name was Desarea Douglas. Her mother had died when she was ten years old, and her world was put into a nose dive from that day on. Her Father had suffered a great deal, and at first he turned to his only child for solace. Then he begin to hit the bottle, and it all fell apart the night he tried to make Desarea his lover instead of daughter. That's the night she spent shivering in her hollow tree.

She had snuck back home after she knew her Father would be at work, and packed almost all her winter clothes, canned food and anything she might need in an emergency. She hauled it three miles down to her tree and slung it from a rope hooked on a knot in side her burrow. She was determined to become self-sufficient.

She was only eleven going on twelve, but had learned about men at an early age from a cousin, and knew she wasn't ready for anything like that at her age

Desarea went to school before her Father was up and she snuck in the house after he passed out from the booze. That meant she walked six miles to and from the house and her tree each school day. Sometimes she spent the night in the hollow tree. She had her sleeping bag, pillow and food and water. The tree was fairly safe from predators, for the simple reason it had an entrance that she barley squeezed through after she took her outer clothes off and threw them in first. She had rolled a rock over from a pile near the trail that descended from the hills. She had balanced it to the left of the entrance hole and after she was in, she rolled the rock in place and it shut ninety-five percent of the hole up.

Her home away home was snug, dry, and almost always warm. She had purchased a huge candle at the store that would burn for months; the candle heated the hollow tree as well.

Food was the only thing she came up short on. Her drunken Father hardly ever brought food home. A couple times she had approached him about this, and all he did was throw some bills at her and go back to his drinking. She always knew what nights he would try to jump in her bed. These were the night's she spent in her tree.

When she turned twelve she had a pretty good handle on things, and had learned what she could or couldn't eat from the forest and hills. In the spring and summer there were more berries and plants then she could eat, she was weary of the little Tennessee Black Bear. It and the Cougar Cat species were what she watched out for. The cats were harder to figure out then the grunting black bear. She could hear the bear coming and get out of its way. One time she ran up on a bob cat, and it scared the heck out of the both of them. The bob cat went screaming off through the bushes, while Desarea froze in place, and almost fainted on the spot. One of the bigger cats came around and snuffed at her covered hole. It must have smelled food, then it tried to dig under the rock, but Desarea said, "SHOO" As loud as she could, and the cat lost all interest in her and in one leap cleared her shield of bushes and was gone. She heard the cat cough from somewhere off in the distance.

Two years of roughing it in the wild, made Desarea as healthy a human species' as could be found on earth. There wasn't one ounce of fat on her body. One day this caused her some concern. At home as she stepped from the shower she saw her reflection in the dirty bath room mirror and was shocked. She was getting fat on her chest. She was growing breast, she realized. Wow, that was really something. She was turning into a woman, and couldn't do one dad burn thing about it. She read books about life and was aware of her change. She was worried her father would notice and intensify his attempts to seduce her. All she could do was to stay out of his way.

One day Desarae came home just before night fell. The house was dark and silent. She went in and stood in the hallway and listened. She looked at her father's bedroom door, and it was open an inch or so. She gently pushed the door open, and saw her dead father half in and half out of bed. She knew he was dead because of his position. No one alive could lay like that for more than a few minutes without falling and busting their butt on the floor.

Desarea sat down on the filthy floor and cried her heart out. She loved her dad even though he had tried to molest her many times; after all she was the image of her mother wasn't she? That's probably what he saw, in his drunken attempts to maul her. She knew she had to inform the authorities of her father's death. First, she went through the house and accumulated all monies. There was quite a lot of it actually and it surprised her. She found her father's wallet on his night stand next to his bed. It was full of hundred dollar bills. She took them out and returned the wallet to its place. First thing she did was go to bed and sleep. When she woke up she took the money and all she could carry to her tree, and then came home and called the 911 operator and told her she thought her father might be dead in his bedroom. The operator become animated and said, "Are you ok honey? Just go outside and wait for the EMT truck and point them to where your father is."

After they took her father away the sheriff talked to Desarea. He wanted to know what she was going to do. She lied through her teeth to the lawman. She said, "I've been staying at my aunt's house in town since mother died and only came out to check on my Father. He drank too much and I think that's what killed him, don't you?"

The deputy had a skeptical look on his face, but he gave her the benefit of doubt, ask her if he could give her a ride to town, a distance of one and a half miles. She declined, saying she must clean the house up some. The deputy felt like he should do something for or about this pretty young girl, he just didn't know what.

After the Deputy left, she got the keys to her father's small Toyota four runner truck. She had spent time watching her father drive the little truck, and thought she could drive it too. She didn't quite understand the gear shift thing, but knew she had to press the clutch in and let it out to make it go. After getting it started she pushed the clutch in, selected a gear and let the clutch out, the little truck took a jump forward, and then stopped suddenly, silent. She pushed the clutch in and restarted the engine once more. Then she saw the other peddle near her right foot and pressed it, the engine roared and unnerved her and she popped the clutch out, and boy they were flying now. She took her foot off the accelerator and the truck idled along peacefully.

She steered it down the dirt road away from the house. When she reached the trail leading to the hollow tree she turned into it. It was narrow but the little truck fit and she idled along in first gear, if the engine begin to labor, she put her foot on the gas peddle and pressed it down, the little truck did ok until it arrived at the creek. There it bogged down and died.

Desarea could see the bushes concealing her tree. She took the Operators book from the glove box and read it. When she came to the four wheel drive part she read it many times so she had a good understanding of how it operated. The hubs were self locking the book told her, she just didn't have the faintest notion of what a hub was. There was a diagram of the two gear shifts, the short one was four wheels drive and high and low range. She moved the lever to the rear and started the engine. A green light in the instrument panel lit up and said FWD. She gassed it and let the clutch out and boy oh boy the little truck literally jumped across the creek. When she finally got it stopped in the bushes surrounding her tree, the truck was hidden so well, anyone would have to come right up on it, to see it.

She really did have an aunt in town, but she was a boozer like her brother and Desarea didn't much care for her or her husband. She had only been around them a few times in her entire life. When she walked in the yard she knew they were here. Their raggedy old car was parked in the drive. She had to face them now. She entered the house, and her aunt Bulla ran to her and engulfed her in an embrace, saying how awful it was, that her dear brother had died in such a horrible way. She smelled like a gin and cigarettes. Desarea disentangled herself, and looked at her aunt with hooded eyes. She appeared much older than she really was, and this set Bulla back a notch. Desarea said slowly, "He drank himself to death, just like you are doing. Get out of my house and stay out. I'll come see you when you sober up."

She was shaking inside, but, appeared calm on the outside. Desarea knew in her heart if she didn't rise up and show some grit now, she would be mopping floors in some foster home, with a shrew of a woman as her tormentor, and an oversexed husband, who took his fill from her and her other foster siblings. She felt something she had never felt in her life until now, it was self-confidence. She believed in herself and no drunk would ever tell her what to do again. She stood as tall as possible and was only an inch shorter than her aunt, who by now had a look of fear in her eyes. Her niece had grown up since she saw her last. She said, "Come on Herman lets go."

Desarea has everything under control here. They left a twelve year old girl shaking so bad she had to sit down or fall down. She was in wonder of herself; she had, by gum pulled it off and her home was still intact, at least for now.

Desarea was sure things would change in the near future, but for now, she was free to study her father's records and maybe figure out what her real situation was. She thought her Father had mentioned paying off the house and five acres of land out of her mother's insurance settlement. She should then, find a deed to the place somewhere. She searched all the places it might be, however all she found was a key with a tag attached by a string. The tag read, First Fed. The young girl hadn't a clue what that meant. She added it to the pile she was collecting to store down in the truck. She knew she didn't want to live in this house, for it hadn't been cleaned since her mom died. She had made attempts, but each time her Father had come up the road in his truck, stopping her cold. She would leave by the back door as he entered the front.

Desarea walked to town to buy non perishables for her hollow tree. As she was walking she looked in all the window fronts. There were all sorts of things she never noticed before. She must be growing up she supposed, last week she was a kid now she was a young woman with some problems. How could she remain where she was before some do-gooder saw through her ruse. Eight month's out of the year in southern Tennessee she could live out doors in her hollow tree, and keep clean in the creek, but January and February can freeze the feathers off a duck, and she shivered to think of a bath in the creek during those two months. It was the fourth of June and she had six months of relatively warm weather before a decision had to be made about that. The more pressing thing was to find out about the house. If it was paid for, she wanted to sell the thing.

As she turned to walk to the dollar store she saw the bank and thought about all the money (over one thousand dollars) she wondered if a twelve year old could do business with a bank. She went on in to the dollar store and came right back out with a surprised expression on her face. She looked at the First Federal Bank on the corner. She had a key to that bank! Then she thought, naa, banks don't give people keys to their banks. It must be a key for a box or something like that. She vowed she would bring the key in and attempt to find out.

Two days later, armed with the key, she hesitatingly entered the bank. A pretty lady in a nice business suit smiled at her, and asked if she could help her. She simple held the key out to the lady, who said, "Oh you want to open your safe deposit box. Ok young lady come with me."

They walked to a room off to the side, and down a set of stairs. At the bottom the lady said, "There you are, sign here and when you finish, come on back up to my desk."

She left Deserea and went back up the stairs. Desarea examined the room. There were rows of small boxes along one wall, and two small rooms on the opposite side. There were numbers on the drawers. She looked at the key and found a number, then looked for the corresponding number on the drawer. Hers was near the back of the room. She inserted the key and turned it. The drawer slid open with no noise. The contents made her gasp. There was row after row of one hundred dollar bills. There was also a packet of papers in one corner, and she looked at those first. There has a hand written will dated about the time her mother had died from cancer. There was also the deed and paid off mortgage on the house. There was an insurance police on her father for 25,000 dollars in case of death from natural causes, or double in case of accidental death. She supposed it might pay up on the natural clause, even if he did drink himself to death. The money must have come from her mother's insurance policy. There was a lot of it. Desarea counted one of the bundles. There was one thousand dollars in it and there were fourteen stacks. Wow! She had a fair bit of money. She had learned to handle money from the bills her drunken Father threw at her from time to time, she learned how far it would go, and how far it didn't go. She knew she was in good shape and there was still the policy on her father, but she didn't have any idea on how to collect it. She supposed she might wait until she was a bit older before trying to cash it in.

There was so much she didn't know, but she was learning fast. She was a sharp kid, and was developed far beyond her twelve years; this was due to her circumstance's at home, and her mother's early death, and with her father's nursing his hurt away on a bottle of whisky. She left everything in the box just like it was, closed it and returned to the banks lobby. The same nice lady said, "Was everything ok honey?"

Desaera bobbed her head and went out the automatic door onto the street. She was shaking and hadn't trusted herself to speak to the nice lady. She took off for home at a dead run.

Desaera went to work on the two bedroom house in earnest now. She cleaned all the windows and floors cleaner than they had been in years. The bath room was a mess. Black grease (her father had been a mechanic) was thick around the tub, and took a lot of back breaking work to clean it. When she finished she hit the kitchen, then the two bed rooms. As she finished her father's room, she heard a knock on the door. It scared the bejebbers out of her. What if it was that deputy again? She looked out the window and saw the electricity company truck, and felt a great relief. She opened the door and the man asked if he could speak to the head of the household.

She almost panicked, but said, "That's me, what can I do for you sir?"

The man said, "You haven't been paying your power bill, and unless you pay it now. I'll have to pull the plug and you will have to pay extra money to have us come and turn it back on."

Desarea asked him how much it was. She had some money in her pocket, but the rest was down in the truck. He held a paper out and pointed to a figure of $79.88 at the bottom of the page. She pulled out a hundred and handed it to him. The lineman damn near lost his bottom lip, his jaw dropped so low. He sputtered that he had no change with him. Desaera went through her pockets once more and found four twenty's and traded them for the hundred dollar bill. She said in a very grown up way, "keep the change."

She had seen that on TV. The service man had a look of respect in his eyes for this young girl. He said, "Thank you very much, try to pay it monthly and we'll all be happy."

She answered, "Yes sir I will." and she meant it too. After he left, Desaera went to the mail box and felt stupid. The thing was so full it was difficult to unload it. She had a full arm load and on the way to the house she turned several times to see if she dropped anything. There was more mail than she could comprehend. She had no notion of what most of it was, but she found a water bill and a bill for her father's funeral. She had forgotten all about him having to be buried. The bill was for $2,698.67. The bill was made out to her dead father. She sat there in wonder. How could you send a bill to a dead man and expect to be paid. She would have to ponder that for some time to come. She supposed she would have to pay it since she had all his money, but there sure wasn't any reason for her to get in a hurry, was there, her Father was dead no matter what.

There were moments when Deserea was riddled with doubt. Here she was not even a teen yet and she had to make adult decisions. She missed being a kid like back before her mother fell sick. First she had had to attend to her mother in the early stages of her illness. Her father was there when not at work. She had ceased being a kid when they took her mother away to the hospital for the last time.

Deserea practiced learning to drive the little Toyota truck every chance she got. She was getting the hang of it and one day drove out on the dirt road and headed south, she had only gone three hundred yards when the little truck up and quit running. She coasted to the edge of the road and stopped under a large tree. She tried to crank the motor. It whinnied like some sick horse but wouldn't hit a lick. She went to the operator's manual to the trouble shooting section, and under engine cranks but will not start. Over to the right under probable cause she saw, out of gas. Check gauge. She looked at the gauge and it said full. She decided to try and crank it once more. When she turned the key on, the fuel gauge went all the way to empty. Her heart fell. What to do.? She raised the hood and prepared to go and find some gas. As she began to walk, an old pickup driven by a much younger woman stopped and said, "Hey, you're just a kid, what are you doing out here alone? Can I give you a lift?"

Deserea thought why not, and she hopped in the truck. The lady asked, "Do you have anything to do with that Toyota truck back there with the hood up"?

Deserea looked at the woman and knew she couldn't lie. The woman reminded her of her mother in some way. She told her the truth. "I was teaching myself how to drive and ran out of gasoline. Now I'm on my way to get some. Can you drop me at a filling station please?"

The woman figured this kid for maybe fourteen and no more. If she had a learners permit, an adult was supposed to ride shotgun with her, but she seemed to have her head on straight. The woman was Arlene Deitman from over in Winepoint, Tennessee, and had been to Knoxville to visit her sick sister. This back route cut ten mile off her trip. The only thing she didn't like about the dirt road was that she had to run the heater fan, and open both wing windows to keep the dust out from the old Chevy pickup. Otherwise it choked her and made her adenoids burn like fire, and she would spit up mud for a week. She said, "Yep, I can sure do that." Almost in the same breath she continued, "Where do you live kid"?

Deserea was silent for just a heartbeat and then said, "Up the road about four miles."

Arlene hoped she would open up more, but Deserea wasn't going to give her any more information about her situation. She felt she had given out too much, as it was.

Arlene turned left at the house and drove the mile and a half to town. She stopped at the filling station on Main Street. Deserea tried to send Arlene on her way at the station, but the woman insisted on bringing her back to the little truck, and helping her get it started. Deserea went in and came out with a three gallon gas can she'd bought, and walked over to the pump. She knew how to do this, just like every thirteen year old in America did. She had done it many times for her Father, back when the family was together and happy. She was almost overcome by sadness and felt like crying. She felt eyes on her, and looked up and locked eyes with Arlene. Arlene saw the sadness in this kids eyes and her heart done a flip. She knew instinctively the girl had been through a lot in her short life, and maybe needed a real friend that wouldn't judge her. With the can of gas paid for and deposited in Arlene's truck they headed back to the Toyota. Arlene attempted to engage Deserea in a fact finding conversation, but the girl answered in mono syllables that weren't helpful. When they turned right onto the dirt road, Deserea didn't dare look up at her house. She wasn't ready to tell this person where she lived and what conditions she lived under. She might report her to some child protection thing or other and her worst nightmare would be realized.

After putting the gas mostly in the tank (some ran on the ground) she got in the driver's seat and turned the starter. The little truck had an electrical fuel pump and it started right up. She left it running and went to talk to Arlene. She thanked her and asked her if she could pay her for her troubles. Arlene said, "No. I was glad to help; can you make it home from here?"

Deserea said, "Yes I can, thank you." She drove the truck another two miles down the road and turned around at a pull off. On her return, she passed the place she had run out of gas and didn't see Arlene anywhere.

Unknown to Deserea, Arlene suspected she lived in the house out on the road at the junction. She parked her old Ford past the house to wait for the girl to return home. It finally grew dark and Arlene supposed she had miscalculated. The girl must live down the dirt road. She reluctantly headed for home, but she was determined to investigate the matter further.

Deserea simply had turned off at the trail that led to her tree, and put the truck back where it was hidden from everyone. It contained all her food and important stuff like money and spare candles and blankets. She had packed the stuff neatly behind the two seats of the extended cab. She thought it might be a bad idea to stay in the house unless it was too cold to stay in her tree, besides; Arlene was much too interested in her for comfort. On top of all that, she loved the tree hollow, it was neater then the old empty house. She had out fitted it with a small FM radio, water jug, and cooking gear of sorts. She needed a cook stove of some type, but didn't know what. Her bed had improved a great deal when she brought a sleeping matt from the house. There was one problem she hadn't worked out yet, and must do so fast. She was getting too big to fit through her entrance hole, especially at her chest. She was going to have big boobs like her mother had, and there was going to come a day when the damn things would prevent her from getting in her burrow. She looked in the truck among her Father's tools, and found an old roofing hatchet. It wasn't much, but she used it to chop the still green tree's hole a bit bigger. The hole was too big now for her door rock, so she selected another one and maintained her 95% closure. She brought some smaller rocks over to the tree and built a small fire ring. She could cook on that from time to time.

As is always the case, when things were perfect, someone had to put their noses in, and foul them up. Deserea grabbed her gas can and headed for town, she wanted the little truck full of gas. It was her security blanket. She could always jump in it and be gone if anything threatening took place. As she approached the highway she was careful not to look at the house in case someone was watching her. After she turned, she was moving fast, almost at a trot. She could go like this for hours if need be. As she approached town, Arlene's Ford pulled up behind her. Arlene's heart was racing. She had started to believe in ghosts when it came to this young lady. Deserea was happy to see Arlene and said, "Hello Arlene how are you?"

Arlene said, "I've been worried about you sweetie. I've looked for your house everywhere and can't find it.

Deserea knew all was lost. This woman held her future in her hands. She made up her mind and said, "OK, let's get some gas, and I'll show you where I live. I need to go to the bank too, before we go to my place." Deserea had all her money in the safe deposit box, and needed some.

Arlene needed to gain this young person trust, her husband of twelve years had died of a heart attack fourteen months ago leaving her childless, and she was lonely for human companionship. she had been fretting for months about her sister down in Knoxville dying of liver cancer, and then she would be all alone in this world. She felt Deserea had some of the same problems she lived with and the two should get to know each other and develop a trust in each other.

When Arlene was directed to turn off on the trail, she couldn't believe what was happening. This girl lived in the woods, and I mean the Woods! The Chevy made it to the creek and Arlene was afraid she would get stuck so she stopped. Deserea talked for a half hour, telling Arlene everything. Finally she said, "If you turn me in to the authorities I wouldn't blame you, but I would never be able to know you then, because they would put me in some foster home where I don't want to be, and I would be lost forever."

She had tears running down her face when she finished. She glanced at Arlene and saw she was crying as well. The two were instantly bonded and in each other's arms. A lot of hurt was let loose from the both of them.

They finally dried their tears and Arlene said, "You are a wonder girl. I don't know of many adults that could have done better. Let's see this hollow tree you mentioned, and by the way where is the Toyota truck parked?"

Deserea said, "Come on I'll show you Arlene."

She sounded like a kid again. Arlene's heart swelled. She led Arlene to the bushes that hid her tree and truck. They were right on the Toyota before Arlene saw it. She said, "WOW you do have it well hidden."

Arlene was too big to go inside the hollow tree, so she stuck her head in and looked around in amazement. She rose up once more and said solemnly; you sure don't belong in any foster home kid, this is absolutely ingenious. I'm floored by what you've done.

They backed the Chevy out to the road and went up to the house. Arlene was impressed by how neat and clean it was. A lot of hard work had gone in to cleaning it up. Arlene was full of questions. "Who paid the bills?"

Deserea said, "I do that's who." She had a grin on her face as she said it.

Arlene said, "WOW, and where does the money come from"? Deserea had held back that part, and was determined to continue to do so.

She said, "I'm pretty good with money and there was quite a lot around the house; it will pay the bills until I sell the house. I just don't know how to sell a house. Maybe you can help me with that?"

She had put it as a question, to see if Arlene agreed with her on selling the house. Arlene chose her words carefully. She said. "Maybe it would be a good idea if you kept this house for the winter. It will get colder than blazes in January you know, you could stay warm here." she added, "There is another option. You could come and stay at my house in Winepoint for the winter, and go to school there."

Deserea was silent for a bit and Arlene let her mull it over. Finally she asked, "Will you ever report me to social services?"

Arlene had tears to spring to her eyes and she hugged the girl as she said, "I may call you my adopted daughter, but no one from any government or state department will ever get their hands on you. You have my promise on that dear girl."

LITTLE BOY LOST

LITTLE BOY LOST
CHAPTER I

The young boy child was fascinated by the butterfly as it fluttered along the ground in a zig zag fashion across the desert and was following it as he stumbled along the desert floor, attempting to catch up with it. The butterfly the boy was chasing, was in actuality, a big moth. The child didn't care one bit; he just loved butterflies, and was determined to catch one. Without realizing it, the boy was going farther and farther from his parent's car, parked at a roadside pull out on route 666, north of Albuquerque New Mexico. The parents, Billy and Teresa Roundman, were sound asleep in the front and rear seats of the old car. They hadn't heard their son Brice open the door, and go out to relieve himself. Brice was six years old and as bright as any child of that age, chasing butterflies excluded. He was like any other child, full of wonder at most things he hadn't had an experience with.

Billy and Teresa were migrant farm workers, and desert dwellers. They lived out of their car, unless they found a job that offered living quarters of sorts. Alcohol was their release from the rigors of life, and they had sat on the side of route 666, consuming the better part of a half-gallon of vodka the night before. When they woke up, they didn't even miss their son. He was still asleep in the floorboard where he always slept as far as they were concerned, when they pulled out and headed south neither thought to check on Brice. They were headed down to pick lemons in Las Cruces, New Mexico.

CHAPTER 2

The scream petrified Billy, who was in the act of reliving himself on a cactus plant at a pullout. He yelled at Teresa, "What's the matter with you woman? You just scared me so bad, I can't pee no more. What's wrong?"

Teresa didn't answer, so he zipped up and walked around to where she was, and what he saw, sent chills through his body. His wife was holding his son's blanket up and staring dumbly at it. He said, "O My god where's Brice?"

His wife fell completely apart then and screeched, "We lost him somewhere, what are we gonna do?"

Billy was numb all over and just sat down on the sand. It felt like a ton of bricks was crushing the breath out of him. Teresa was the first to react in a positive manner. She grabbed her husband and literally stuffed him in the driver's side of the car, then, jumping in she said, "Drive!" He must have gotten out to use the bathroom back where we spent the night. We will find him there."

She said the last with a plaintive note in her voice. They had traveled for four hours, after spending the night at the road side. The problem was, there were many of those road side pullouts, and they more or less all looked the same.

CHAPTER 3

Little boy Brice lost the butterfly and decided to return to the car he called home. He took off in what he thought was the way back to the highway, but it was exactly the opposite direction. He never thought to follow his footsteps back to the road. He was fully dressed, because he always slept in his clothing, as did his mother and father. He had on Nike shoes his mother had found almost new at the Salvation Army thrift store, when they were working in California picking peaches last summer. His Jeans were Tuff Nut brand and were almost new. He had a T shirt on that read; "World's Greatest Son". There was a picture of the sun blazoned on to the front background of the garment. He was a good looking boy and big for his age. Most people thought him to be eight or nine not six. He was inquisitive by nature and soon found other things to interest him, He found what looked like a track left by someone dragging a large rubber hose though the sand. He followed the track and soon came up on a huge lizard. It was ugly and had hardly any tail, just a blunt stub. He had been cautioned by his dad, that some snake like things in the desert were deadly. The Gila monster turned and confronted this intruder with a loud hiss. This caused Brice to back pedal a pace or two. After a while, ole ugly took off and Brice let him. He didn't seem too friendly anyhow. The sun was overhead and he was no closer to the car, than when he started. He was thirsty and hungry, but as he turned all four directions he saw nothing but desert and nothing to eat or drink. He was getting scared now and sat on a rock and cried. He missed his mom and dad terribly and wished he hadn't chased that butterfly.

CHAPTER 4

Billy broke the speed limit all the way back to where they thought Brice might be. Every one of them pullout things looked the same. He couldn't pinpoint the one they spent the night at. He turned to his wife and told her they would have to stop at every last one and circle around away from the stop on both sides of the road in case their son had crossed the deserted highway.

They had been at it for two hours when Teresa yelled that she had found her sons foot prints and took off at a run following them. Billy yelled at her and said, "Honey we have to take food and water with us. We will need it, and so will our son when we find him."

This made sense to Teresa, and she turned and ran back to the car. Billy noticed his son's prints. They were zig zaging all over the place, like he was chasing something. He hoped it wasn't a poisonous something. Teresa came back with a gallon of water, canned beef and bread. They began tracking their son, and topped over a small hill and lost sight of the car and road. The tracks of their son went around in a circle and then lined out west, the opposite direction of the car. The boy's track had much more purpose now, Billy noticed whatever his son had been chasing had either escaped or his son had caught it.

CHAPTER 5

Brice grew tired as the sun began its dive to the west. He came up on a small dip in the desert and went down and rested with his back against a bunch of rocks. It was warm down here and he soon dozed in the late sunshine. Something woke him. He looked down and saw a small puppy trying to take a bite out of his Nike shoe. The little Coyote was hungry and the rubber smelled like food to him, and he was determined to get some. Brice reached down and picked the pup up, He received a nip on his finger. He cuffed the pup and then petted it. The pup responded with affection and snuggled in his lap. Brice began to hear other noises from inside the rock pile and pretty soon more pups came out to where Brice and the pup sat. Before long, he had six pups in his lap snuggled down asleep. He heard a noise at the rim of the indention, and looked up into the eyes of mama coyote. The female was growling way back in her throat. This almost scared the pee out of Brice. He knew wild animals didn't take well to anyone messing with their young, but the pups had more or less adopted him. He picked one of the whelps up and sat it on the ground away from him. The pup let out a howl and scampered right back and snuggled in and went back to sleep. Mama coyote stopped growling and just looked at the boy through soft brown eyes. She didn't perceive any threat from this creature and her pups were fine with it. The prime motive for the mama was the safety of her off spring and as far as her pea sized brain could reason out;

they were safe with this whatever it was. She took up a position at the rim of the den and put her snout on her front paws and watched the six pups and one strange being. After a while she closed her eyes and slept, something she wasn't able to do much of when the pups slept with her, because one of them always needed attention, and it kept her awake.

Brice was awakened by the sun in his eyes and the pups deserting his lap to go and squat and pee or whatever. He looked up where the Female had been and there was no sign of her. He knew he had been granted permission to stay here, as one of the family of coyotes. The desert was really cold at night during the winter months. Brice had been kept warm by six hot little puppies during the night. Now he was some kind of thirsty. He remembered his dad talking about finding water in the desert. Something about a barrel cactus having water you could squeeze out from its insides. All he had to do was get inside one of the cactuses that dotted the desert. He went up over the rim and saw a cactus near the den. He took a good sized rock from a pile, and hit the cactus on its round top. It was one tough thing, but with perseverance, he finally broke through the outer layer and removed the hook thorns that covered the thing. He reached down inside the cactus and withdrew a large hand full of pulp that resembled the honey dew melons his mother fed him from time to time. The stuff felt wet, so he squeezed it above his mouth and was surprised that a stream of bitter water dribbled out of it. He reckoned it wouldn't kill him, so he grabbed another hand full and repeated the process. He was just putting the rock over the wound to his cactus, when he noticed the mother coyote sitting a few feet away with a bird of some sort in her mouth. The boy jumped back in the den and assumed his spot. The coyote landed lightly near him and walked over and dropped the desert chicken (grouse) at his feet and returned to the rim of her den and put her snout on her paws. Brice picked the bird up and felt its warmth; it was a very fresh kill. Brice had helped dress chickens with his grandma out in Oklahoma and this was just a smaller version. He pulled the brown and white feathers from the chest and then skinned the big breast. He ripped one of the breast halves out and took a bite of it. He was hungry enough that it tasted good. He ripped the other out, and took one more bite but he was full, he then began to feed the pups small bits. He pinched the organs into many pieces and the pups fought over each morsel. When most of the meat was gone, the coyote jumped down and took the remains of the bird topside and Brice could hear bones being crunched to small pieces and consumed. When the Mama coyote was finished, she leaped back in the den, and groomed her pups. When she finished with them, she approached Brice and began matter of factly licking his face clean of bird blood and then did the same to his dirty hands. Brice was amazed that he wasn't one bit scared. This wild animal had adopted him into her clan without any reservations whatsoever.

CHAPTER 6

Billy and Teresa walked as fast as possible following the boy's footprints. Sometimes the prints disappeared and they had to circumnavigate until they found them once more. This all took time and before long the sun was below the horizon, and it began to grow dark. Billy finally told his wife they needed help finding their son. Teresa slumped to the ground and began to sob loudly. Billy took her in his arms and consoled her. He said with more conviction then he felt, "Our son isn't a dummy and I think he will be alright until tomorrow, let's go and get help at the sheriff's department, they will get a helicopter out here at first light and in short order we will have our boy back,"

The two walked east until the road came in sight. Their old car was being inspected by a state policeman. They ran to the car. Teresa began talking while they were a good hundred feet from the officer. She had tears streaming down her face and was more or less incoherent. The trouper pulled his sidearm and said, "Stop right there and put your hands where I can see them." The two stopped dead and put up their hands.

Billy grew just a little PO'ed at this unnecessary precaution. Even an idiot could see they were distraught and not criminals bent on doing the cop any harm. Billy said, "We have lost our son in the desert and need help finding him before he freezes to death."

The cops face grew red in the light of his head lights and as he lowered his gun, he apologized, asking how long the boy had been in the desert. They told the trooper the entire story, leaving out the almost half gallon of vodka the two had consumed the night before. The policeman got on the radio and said he wanted a lot of bodies out here ready to kick off at first light. He ordered a helicopter to fly this way at dawn also. He tried to get the couple to go back to Albuquerque and get some rest, but both of them were adamant that they would remain here in case the boy made it back. The cop was sympathetic now and knew they were right and if they remained here he wouldn't have to.

CHAPTER VII

Morning found a bee hive of activity around the old dodge car. twenty or so men showed up with five more troupers. They heard the helicopter before they saw it, sounding like some kid slapping the water with a paddle in their pool. The trooper put his arms out in the direction the prints went. There was a bunch of prints now that Billy and Teresa had walked it twice. The chopper had no problem following the trail. Within minutes it arrived back and set down. The pilot talked to the ranger in charge and then he took off for town. The trooper came to the couple. He said, "The chopper has developed some mechanical problems. The pilot felt it was safer to return to base and repair it, and then come back later today. We will search on foot, and I'm sure we'll find your son today."

The contingent of searchers spread out one hundred feet apart, and walked west. The cop in charge and the parents took the center and Billy being part Indian, assumed the position of tracker. The tracks weren't always clear. When they came to rock, Billy had to guess which direction to take. When the line of men and one woman reached the rock formation where the Coyote den was hidden, Billy had not seen a clear track for twenty minutes and consequently, missed the den by a good two hundred yards. The man on the far right looked at the rock formation, but it was too far over to possibly hide the boy.

CHAPTER 8

Brice had never eaten raw jack rabbit before, but it tasted good to the half starved boy. The Mother Coyote had dropped the fresh killed rabbit on the ground in front of the Boy and Pups. They all seven tore at the carcass, and Brice was the one to referee, making sure everyone got his or her share. When Mama felt they had eaten their share, she took the remains to the rim of the den, and consumed all they left that was edible, including bones.

Brice had heard the helicopter, but by the time he was able to climb out of the den, it turned and left the way it had come. He stood there with tears streaming down his cheeks. He felt a sense of loss no child should have to experience. Where were his dad and mom? They surely had missed him by now, and why did the chopper turn around?

The Mama Coyote saw all the activity spreading out from the old car on the highway, and knew the strange addition to her family came from that car. She was neutral in her feelings about the new critter. It was accepted by her offspring and that was all that mattered to her. Yet she knew something wasn't right, the critter didn't belong here with her and her pups. She elected to take things as she saw them, and decided to help things along. She knew the searchers had missed her den by a narrow margin, and they would be returning before long, and might discover her den and harm her natural born pups. She nuzzled the boy out of the den, and up on to the desert. Each time the boy attempted to go the wrong way, she steered him towards the car. They finally came in sight of it, and the coyote sat down. Brice saw the deserted car and started to run, and then stopped and turned to the coyote, she held eye contact with him. He said softly, "Thank you," and waved his hand. The Coyote turned and at a dead run went back to her unprotected pups.

CHAPTER 9

As Brice approached the car he heard the helicopter coming once more. He looked up as it hovered a short distance away. He saw the pilot talking on the radio microphone in an excited way. The chopper sat down and the pilot came over to Brice. He noted his clothing was filthy with some kind of blood, but his face and hands were clean. He said, "Hello son, are you OK?"

Brice looked at him and asked; "Do you know where my mother and father are?"

The pilot told him they were out looking for him, and would be here soon. He asked the boy, "How did you make it fella, almost three days in the desert and your face is still clean? How did you keep warm at night?, the temperature has been below freezing the two night's you spent out there."

Brice felt he only wanted to share that story with his mother and father and not some stranger, it was too personal.

When the radio call came through that Brice had made his way back to the car, Billy and Teresa were ready to run all the way back, but the deputy told them; I'll have the chopper pick you up. He made the call and they heard it coming before it came in sight. In the right front seat sat Brice. There was a joyful reunion of the three. Billy turned his nose up and jokingly said, "Boy you smell like a wolf den."

Brice asked his dad, "Is a wolf anything like a coyote dad?"

Billy thought, oh my god, his son had been taken in by coyotes, surer than all get out. That explained the clean face and hands. The boy should have frozen to death in only a "T" shirt. The Coyotes kept him warm and fed him wild uncooked game. That explained the dried blood on his clothing. Billy was extremely proud of his son. The boy had found a way to survive, where most folks would have died. He asked his son, "How did you find your way back to the car?"

Billy already knew the answer. Brice said, "The Mama coyote brought me back. I think she was protecting her young, because she knew you were searching for me and if you found me it would put her puppies in danger."

Billy was completely astounded by his son. The boy seemed to have matured noticeably since he last saw him. Teresa wouldn't let go of him, Brice didn't mind one bit.

Chapter 10

The choppers took the deputy and the family back to the car, and were met by more reporters and cameras than thought possible out here. Someone had picked up the choppers call and at break neck speed, arrived just as the chopper landed. They tried to corner the boy, but Teresa rushed him to the car and locked the door. Billy confronted the reporters. They asked so many questions it was impossible to answer even one. Billy held his hands up, until the group stood silent, and then he said, "My son was saved by some wild animals in the desert and we will tell the story at some later date. We will go to a motel in Albuquerque and you can contact us there. Right now we need our privacy."

The Deputy ran interference for the family. He told the reporters that he knew this was a great story and someone had better be prepared to pay for it. He said, "Think about that on your way back to town."

The story hit Routers the next day, the boy had told all for a price. Respect for the sly Coyote rose to a new high around the country and Billy, Teresa and Brice left town in a brand new Toyota twenty-two foot motor home, that was tagged, titled, and fully insured and; Brice had his own bed to sleep in for the first time in his young life.

LOSS OF INNOCENCE

LOSS OF INNOCENCE

The sixteen year old girl didn't know what to think about what she saw. She had grown up in a north Kansas, City suburb, and until today, had never seen anything to equal the sight of, what at first seemed to be total chaos, but in fact, was years and years of purposeful neglect, on the part of the farmer. Old tractors, implements, beat up trucks, and pure junk, were scattered everywhere. The porch on the front of the white frame farm house was falling down, and, trying to drag the rest of the house with it.

The girl's name was Seselia Dawn Prestly. She was a run-a-way. Her father and mother didn't have any idea, where their little girl was, and really down deep, didn't care one way or the other. She had been a hand full since turning two years old anyhow. Head strong and self opinionated, she had had her way in most things for her entire life, but this was one big step, even for her. She had responded to an ad in the Kansas City Farmers friend newspaper, that came free to most homes in Kansas City. A farmer near Independence Kansas had Horses and needed a young girl to work on the farm, and take care of them.

The add stated, room and board was included in the package, along with spending money. Seselia had loved horses all her life, and when she read the alluring ad in the paper, her hormones went wild. She put the paper down and began to day dream about riding horses all day every day.

Days went by, and she became much more embittered towards her parents. They were pretty much hooked on the slogan, "it must be five o'clock somewhere", thing and could be found in front of the T.V. with a tall glass of Tom Collins in their hand. It was a simple matter to slip away from home. Both her Mom and Dad worked during the day, and came home at seven P.M. after visiting the local Bar, only to continue their drinking on into the night.

They didn't miss their daughter for three days, On Saturday morning, it was normal for the family to have breakfast together. Seselia's Mother, Dorothy left her bed at eight A.M. and went into the kitchen, and begin preparations for the meal. Normally Seselia came down, and helped her mother with fixing the meal, this was the only mother and daughter get together of the week, but this morning she missed coming down, and Dorothy went to her room and found it deserted. She knew her daughter had taken flight, she could tell from the way clothing were thrown about the room. Seselia was a clean neat person, and would never leave her room in such a mess if she had any intentions of ever coming back. Dorothy sat down on her Daughter's bed and cried her eyes out. She cried for all the lost years at the bottom of a bottle of booze.

She hadn't even drank when she met Seselia's father. He introduced her to alcohol after the kid was born, and she had been in an alcoholic misty haze ever since.

Dorothy finished her cry and went down stairs to tell her husband Dodger, their Daughter was missing. Dodger was suffering from a gigantic hangover and at first, didn't comprehend what his wife was saying. When it finally hit his brain that his Daughter was really missing, he said," I think she's been missing for some time Dorothy, and maybe we should just let hard knocks teach her a few lessons."

Dorothy flopped on the couch and begab to wail like a big cat. Dodger couldn't take anymore, and lit out for his work shop, where he had a bar set up. He was off on a week end drunk now for sure.

CHAPTER 2

Seselia made her way to Independence Kansas with her thumb. Every ride she caught was from men by themselves, and it worried her. She had never done such a thing before. Her first ride dropped her in Iola Kansas. She hadn't been standing with her thumb out for more than a minute when a young guy not too much older than her, stopped and picked her up. As she slid into the truck seat, she could feel his eyes on her. She looked at him and he had a hot look in his eyes. Seselia was scared half to death, but finally stared him down. He finally dropped his eyes and said he was only going as far as Chanute Kansas, and she was welcome to ride. Her last ride was the really hairy one. The ride before had dropped her at county road two thousand fifty four off U.S. hi-way seventy-five, a few miles from Independence, Kansas She walked down the gravel road lugging her bag. It finally got too heavy and she set it on the road side and dropped down on it. As she reflected on the past few days, she saw a white pickup turn off seventy-five onto her road. She stood up as it approached her. She didn't even stick her thumb up, because she felt bad vibes from the driver of that truck. She turned away, but the truck stopped anyway. Seselia felt like running, but there was really no place to go. She finally turned around and confronted the driver. He was an older man and smiled at her, and said," Hello, can I offer you a ride?"

The man was smiling, but his light blue eyes were cold and looked right through her. Seselia couldn't help but shiver, even though the temperature was in the low eighties. She really didn't want to get in the truck, but she needed a ride and as far as she could tell this back country road wasn't flooded with traffic. She threw her suitcase in the seat and stepped in and closed the door. At least she had a barrier of sorts between her and this man, and if worse came to worse, she would bail out and leave her belongings behind.

The man appeared to be in his sixties and was dressed in farm clothes. Seselia noticed a smell like something dead in the truck. She had smelled the same thing on the hi-way from time to time, and her father had told her it was pig crap. She rightly assumed this man was a pig farmer. She convulsed at the thought and shook her head to get rid of the image that suddenly sprang into her head.

The first words he spoke after they were under way, scared the pee out of her, he said, "My, but you are a fine looking young lady. I have a girl coming down from Kansas City to work for me, and look after my two horses. I sure hope she looks as good as you do."

Seselia came close to jumping out of that truck right then and there. Her heart tried to jump out of her chest. She finally stuttered, "Are you Mr. Snow?"

The man replied, "Why yes I am. How did you know?"

She replied, "Oh just a lucky guess I suppose. Mr. Snow I don't think this will work out. My name is

Seselia Prestly and I sent you my résumé, and you called me and told me to come on down, but I am not a pig farmer at all, and I think I should forget this crazy idea and just go Home"

Talbert Snow didn't say anything for a bit, then he said, "I'll tell you what, you come take a look, and if you don't want to stay, I'll take you back to town. OK? "

She said, "I guess so."

CHAPTER 3

Now here she stood and wondered if she dared even consider staying near this man. He really freaked her out with his eyes and peculiar disarming smile. He took her across the road to show her the two horses, Buck and Billy. He told her to stay away from Billy, because he was a one man horse that he'd caught out in the Sierra Mountains, and brought here to Kansas with him. She was welcome to mount the one named Buck any time she felt like. The way he said it gave her the willies and almost caused her to change her mind once more. She petted old Buck and was lost forever in this sweet old palomino horse. Talbert showed her the tack room in the barn, and where to get feed and hay for the two animals He then took her across to the mobile home at the south end of the old farm house. He told her this would be her home. After Talbert Snow left, Seselia sat down at the kitchen table, and had a good cry. She missed her Mother and home more than she thought she would. Soon she felt better and started to take notice of her surroundings. The place wasn't in the best of repair and not too cleans either. There was hot water and dish soap to clean with. She flew into cleaning the place up. Two hours later it didn't look like the same house. If the wind blew from across the road where the fairing houses were, the smell would knock you off your feet, she would make the best of it, for as long as she could, and if it got too bad, she could leave.

The next few days were uneventful for the runaway girl. She was up each day with the chickens, and out doing chores all around the farm. The only thing she found so far to like about the dilapidated farm was old Buck. He nickered at her each time she approached the pasture he and Billy had the run of. Billy was a bit standoffish at first, but each day that passed, he moved a little closer to Buck and Seselia. The horse and girl were becoming best friends, and old Billy was not as much a one man horse, as Talbert Snow thought he was. Towards the end of that first week, Billy, finally threw all caution to the wind, and came up to Seselia and Buck and nuzzled Seselia's arm. The rest was a thing of beauty to see. The horse had been alone way too long because of the stigma, Farmer Snow had implanted in each person's mind that the horse was mean and nasty. The girl had two friends on the farm now.

Days later, she noticed farmer Snow, watching the three of them as he made his rounds on his tractor. When she looked at him, he quickly turned his head away from her. Seselia thought this was strange behavior coming from an old man. She didn't want to make trouble. She forgot about it and went back to work.

That evening late, there was a gentle knock on the mobile home door. Seselia answered in her night wear. Talbert Snow, ask if he could come in. She said she was sorry, but she was on her way to bed. He stood there much too long for Seselia's liking. Finally, he simply turned and walked away, Saying goodnight as he left. Seselia was shaking like a leaf and found it a chore, closing and locking the door. She knew she had to leave this evil feeling place as soon as possible. She vowed she would leave at first light.

Sometime in the night she heard strange noises from outside the trailer. She thought it might be small animals. She had seen evidence of them everywhere on the farm. She went back into a troubled sleep, and dreamed Talbert Snow was chasing her through Buck and Billy's paddock. Buck and Billy were trying to bite Talbert Snow on the ass. The dream left her soaking wet with sweat, and shaking badly. She decided to get ready to leave this place. After packing her things she opened the door and there was Billy and Buck, with nose bags on, munching on grain and tied to her living quarters. She dropped her bag and set down in the door and cried her eyes out. She loved these two horses with all her heart, and knew she could not possible leave them.

Little did Seselia realize farmer Snow had coldly and calculatingly used Billy and Buck, to keep her on the farm. She let her heart over rule her better judgment and unpacked her clothing. Talbert Snow was there when she came out. He said, "Good morning, I thought you might want to ride Buck and lead Ole Billy out on the road this morning." Seselia knew then, she had been snookered by this, whatever he was person.

Seselia dodged Talbert as much as possible, and worked at anything she found to do. Talbert didn't bother her anymore. She hitched a ride to

Independence, and bought food to eat, with the paltry bit of money, Farmer Snow turned loose of.

One morning, as she exited her trailer, Talbert Snow was waiting for her. He said, "You have been working real well girl, and I think you can help me with the pigs now."

Seselia bucked up at him and said, "Mr. Snow, I told you when I came here, I was not a pig farmer, and you said all I had to do was look after your horses. I've done much more than that, and I'll do much more, but I will not slop your hogs for you."

Talbert Snow had been a predator of young girls for many years, and knew how to manipulate them in almost any situation that arose. He knew the horses were the key to bending this beautiful girl to his will, and he wasn't afraid to use them. He told Seselia, all you have to do is ride Buck each morning and stop off where I'm filling the hog feeders and tie Buck to a tree in the shade. She could then operate the fill chute for him as he drove from feeder to feeder. It would take two to three hours and would help him a great deal, because he had a bad knee and it hurt him to get off and on the tractor. Seselia felt defeated and told him O.K. she would do that for him, but she needed more pay at the end of the week. Talbert had a guarded look on his face, when he said, "We'll see how you go."

All that week, Seselia worked as hard as she could, to try and fit in with the operation. Friday arrived, and this was payday as well. When the farmer handed her an envelope with her pay, she stuck it in her jumper pocket, and forgot about it. She assumed wrongly, that Talbert Snow was a fair man. She didn't open the envelope until she was in town, at the store. That devil had added five dollars, to the ten she normally received. She knew it was not going to work. She stuffed the measly fifteen dollars in her jean pocket and caught a ride back to the farm, packed her bag and tried to open the door to leave. It wouldn't open; the evil person had locked her in from the outside. With pounding heart, she ran to the rear door, and found it locked as well.

Seselia, wanted to scream, but she knew it was wasted energy. No one would hear her. The road running by this farm was little used, and the nearest neighbor lived two miles down the road. She yelled at the farmer, "You won't get away with this. I called my mother and she is coming to pick me up."

She hoped this out and out lie would make him let her go. "If you don't open this door, you will go to jail, you mean old man you." Seselia broke down crying at this point.

Talbert Snow heard every word Seselia said and it did worry him a bit, enough so, that he decided he would do nothing tonight, in case the mother did arrive to pick the girl up. He had plenty of time to execute his plans for the girl later. He went in his house and watched television, then went to sleep.

Back at the mobile home, Seselia tried each window, but they were of the type that had three eight inch Panes in them and somehow the farmer had locked them so she could not open them, all she could do is break them out. After hours of procrastination, she did exactly that. She took one of the heavy kitchen chairs, and threw it at one of windows in the living room. Glass flew everywhere, she picked the chair up and slammed it into the window once more, this time the results, were much more dramatic. The entire window fell outside, and there was her escape hole. She grabbed her packed bag, and threw it through the opening. She let herself down with caution on to the broken glass. As she let go of the window opening and turned to leave, Talbert Snow grabbed her from behind, causing her most feared nightmare to be realized. She screamed at top volume, before he clamped his hand over her mouth. Seselia was amazed at the strength of this slight old man. She knew she had only a few moments to fight this animal off. She began to kick and scratch him with her one free hand. She bit one of his fingers and tasted blood. Her assailant removed his hand from her mouth and she broke away from him. He had a hand full of clothes however and ripped her 'T' shirt right off. All she had on was a bra. This seemed to only increase his efforts to take her by force. He hit her with his fist and knocked her half out. She was lying on the ground, and he had removed her jeans by the time she fully regained her facilities. It was too late to stop him. He raped her repeatedly over the next few hours. She remembered feeling like one of his sow pigs. At last, his ardor cooled and he left her there, and went to his house. He returned in one of his old trucks and told her to get dressed, and he would take her into town. She could get the morning bus to Kansas City.

Seselia felt dirty, used up and ashamed. Like a zombie, she dressed in a clean "T" shirt and some jeans, and then she climbed in the back of the truck. Talbert Snow tried to make her get in the front, but she flat refused. She knew better than to enter that truck cab with that monster in it. She knew she wouldn't go to the police and she knew the Farmer knew it too. It was her word against his, as to whether it was consensual sex or rape.

What Seselia didn't realize, was, that if she had gone to the police as soon as she was dropped off at the Greyhound bus depot, Talbert Snow would have been arrested right after the medical exam, and would have spent many years in jail, not on his farm, taking advantage of more unsuspecting young girls, who's only vice, was loving horses.

MURDER IN QUITMAN COUNTY

MURDER IN QUITMAN COUNTY
Real Fiction.
But More Likely, An Out And Out Lie.

Daulton Ramsey was bare backed, red in the face and sweating like a cold jug of Cider on a hot day. The work he was doing on this hot day in May in southwest Georgia wasn't easy or much to his liking, but his wife of sixteen years, Sally, wanted a flower garden without rocks in it and he was digging down three feet and removing all of the rock and putting them in a big pile. The pile was getting bigger and bigger and Daulton was feeling hotter and hotter, when his spade struck metal with a dull ring.

Daulton dug around the object until he unearthed it and picked it up. It was an old double barrel shotgun with all the wood rotted off it. Daulton could see it had once been a nice gun but now rust had taken all that nice away and left a piece of junk behind.

Daulton needed a break from his labors so he took the gun in to show his wife. He told her, "I'll just bet you someone was shot and killed with this old piece and the killer buried it in that garden spot."

Sally looked pale and said, "Oh my God, I'll bet your right Hon. I wonder who it was, this house has been in my family since the seventeen hundreds. Maybe you should put it back in the ground and not take a chance."

Daulton looked at his wife. She was serious as a mad dog loose and had eyes as large as lemons. He said, "Look Hon, if someone was murdered by that gun, then we are bound by law to report it to the proper authorities. Maybe I'll take it over to Sonny Burns in the morning and see if maybe he'll have some insight about it."

With that Daulton laid the old gun on the kitchen counter and went back to work in the flower bed, after getting all those damn rocks out he still had to visit Wall-Mart, to buy dirt to replace the rocks he was breaking his back to extract from the earth.

CHAPTER 2

Sometime Daulton had a hard time sleeping at night. He would sleep for three or four hours and then wake up and not be able to return to slumber for the remainder of the night. He would slip from the bed and go play with his computer until Sally woke up at six am. It had taken twenty seven bags of dirt to fill that damn hole he made in Sally's garden and by the time he was done his ass was flat dragging the ground. He went straight to the shower. Sally had dinner on the table and after eating; Daulton laid his tired body down on the day bed in the living room and went sound asleep. Sally turned the TV off and threw a cover over Daulton, she felt guilty about having him work so hard on his day off. She then went off to bed.

Dalton's eyes popped open. He looked over at the clock on the TV and saw it was 203 AM. Something woke him up from an exhausted sleep. He heard it once again, it came from the kitchen. Daulton reached for the 357 magnum pistol he kept in the drawer by the bed. He came to his feet and cocked the gun all in a fluid motion and took a step towards the kitchen. Then he noticed a bluish glow coming from there and the hair stood up on his back and neck. He took another giant step to the kitchen entrance and took in a sight that scared the pee out of him and caused his bowles to feel loose and he came near to filling his fruit of the looms. Daulton was not a coward, but what he saw in his kitchen, defied anything in the real world, he had ever seen.

Three ghostly figures stood around the kitchen counter where the rusty old shotgun lay. One was an old man in overalls and white shirt. He was bare headed, with thin gray hair. The other two, were a beautiful wild haired young woman and a strapping light skinned buck Negro in slave clothing. They seemed to be arguing among themselves over the gun. This really spooked Daulton and caused him to take a short back step, and in doing so, his foot slapped the floor. The three ghosts, evaporated in an instant, leaving Daulton shaking from both fear and cold. The windows were all open and it was damn chilly. That was his story and he was a gonna stick to it by damn.

Sally woke up at 558 am, went to the bathroom and then to the kitchen. She always found Daulton there each morning. This morning he seemed different somehow. She kissed him good morning and asked him how his night had been? He looked at her and said, "You're not going to believe me when I tell you"

Sally got a scared look on her face and said, "My god what happened?"

Daulton said, "We have three ghosts in our house".

He related the incident to his wife and when he finished, Sally jumped up, grabbed the rusty gun, opened the back door and with all the strength she could muster, slung the thing out in to the back yard. Daulton said, "Holy jumped up Jessy, what did you do that for dear heart?"

Sally, out of breath and red in the face, sat down and said, "That old man ghost you described was my Grandfather. He died right here in this house when I was a little girl, and I would just as soon he stayed that way, thank you."

Daulton laughed out loud and then realized his wife was sincere and was honestly in fear of those ghosts.

Daulton didn't know if he was scared or not. He thought he was more curious then frightened by what he had seen. Then he realized by bringing that old piece of crap into the house, he had invited three ghosts into their home. The gun; had to have been used to murder the beautiful young woman and the Buck Negro slave and the murderer had to be Sally's Grandfather. Man, what a mess.

Daulton could come up with all kinds of reasons why his Grandpa in law killed those two, but in his heart he knew why. The two committed hanky panky, and got caught, and back then a shotgun was the choice weapon of the executioner. For a black man and white woman caught in the act of fornicating with each other, certain death was the only cure. The old man had probably been completely within his rights to dispatch the two to their graves

.

CHAPTER 3

Sally went to work, and Daulton threw the rusty gun in the back of his truck. He crossed the bridge into Alabama, and turned right onto US highway 431 north, Ten minutes later, he parked at Sonny's Bait Shop. He had known old Sonny his whole life and Sonny never seemed to change. He had lived here all his seventy years and had never gotten more than a hundred miles from home. He dabbled in guns and knew a lot more about them then most folks gave him credit for.

Daulton walked in with the shot gun in his hand and there was noone there, but a bell had chimed when he entered and old Sonny shouted from out back. "Good morning, I be with you in a moment."

Sonny came out with a smile and said, "Hi Daulton long time no see."

He shook Daulton's hand. The old man's grip was firm and dry and he seemed genuinely glad to see Daulton. Sonny looked down at the gun in Daulton's hand and asked, "What that you got in your hand Daulton?"

Daulton held the gun out to Sonny and the old black re-coiled like the gun was a snake. The whites of Sonny's eyes were showing and he said, "Where'd you get that thing Daulton?"

Daulton was surprised by his reaction. He said, "I dug it up in Sallie's new flower garden, out at the house."

Sonny said, "Oh, my lord."

Then he set down on one of the chairs gathered about a potbelly stove in the corner of the room. The old guy was pretty shook up and shaking all over. "Bad." He said, "I sure could use a drink of whisky right now, but there's not been a drop around here for twenty years."

Daulton put the gun down on the floor and said. "I'll be right back Sonny!" He remembered there was a full bottle of Canadian club whiskey behind his Truck seat. When he came back, he handed the bottle to sonny and said, "Here my friend."

He set down facing the old man as; Sonny uncapped the whiskey and took a long pull on it. Daulton said," sonny, you need to tell me what's going on, "I had that old gun lying on my kitchen counter last night and three ghosts were moving the damn thing down the counter top, then I disturbed them and caused them to disappear into thin air. You know something so give."

Sonny pulled on the bottle once more.

CHAPTER 4

Sonny got up and went behind the counter to a pop cooler. He grabbed two cold Pepsi's. He walked back over and handed one to Daulton, then sat down once more. He said, "Oh my lord, I don't know where to begin. The old folks use to tell this story around the fire late at night and as a little boy I heard it many times but didn't know if it was true or not until today. I think maybe it is now, you found the gun mentioned in the story. Man oh Man this is rough on this old man but I tell you best I can."

Sonny said, "It started way back in eighteen fifty nine. Your wife's Grandfather ordered a mail order bride from half-starved Ireland. Maybe that was her reason for becoming one, no one could quite figure out why she needed to go and become a mail order bride. She must have had many young men seeking her favors where she was born. Maybe she just wanted to come to American and chose that method to do it. Your wife's Grandfather was Hershel Don Willis and he was twenty eight years old when his bride to be, Maisey Jo Ann Pitford, stepped off the boat in New York City. Maisey was seventeen years old and one hell of an eye full. When she walked down the gang plank, all heads swiveled around to watch this beautiful girl disembark. Herchel's heart swelled and he felt proud of his decision to mail order a bride. He approached Maisey and saw she had made a sign with a crayon. It read, "Herchel's Maisey". She could have had buck teeth and be cross eyed and it wouldn't have mattered after that.

He would still have loved her. When Hershel stood in front of her, she smiled at him and taking hold of her skirt with both her thumbs and fore fingers she curtsied as prettily, as if he were her King. Hershel took her right hand in his and returned the honor. He asked, "Are you ready to go home my love?"

Maisey said, "Yes sir."

The wedding was held on Sunday June fourth, 1859, at the George Town Church of God on the banks of the Chattahoochee River. The church was filled to capacity, because Hershel was an important cotton grower in the area. He treated his slaves well and they worked well for him. Only white folk attended the church service but, all of Herchel's blacks surrounded the little Church. The wedding was the social event of the year, and a huge picnic was planned for after the wedding. Much celebrating would take place far into the night. The newlyweds went home, shut themselves in and consummated their marriage.

CHAPTER 5

Life settled down for the two newlyweds. Maisey was a perfect bedroom partner and Hershel wanted it to go on forever. He was desperately in love with this Irish lass. She seemed to get along with all the household help and was a happy well-adjusted young girl. Hershel was gone most days overseeing his vast cotton plantation. He grew 2500 acres of cotton on 3000 acres of land. His Father and Grandfather had farmed this same grant of land since the early 1700s and it was a neat well maintained property."

Sonny was silent for a bit, and then he continued, "Back in them days it was common for slave owners to cover their slave girls, but Hershel didn't believe in that. As a matter of fact he felt blacks belonged to blacks and white to white and he expected the blacks to abstain from fornication unless they were duly married by him. Maybe that will help you understand what happened next."

"A year of bliss went by and the two seemed to be happy together. Maisey had a fiery temper and every once in a while it flared up. Hershel would let her vent her anger on him to a certain point and then say, "That's enough Maisey."

She would look at him and her anger would disappear as quick as it came and things went back to normal. She would once again become the loving wife he married.

CHAPTER 6

Hershel had happy slaves. They were not over worked, and were fed and clothed as well as possible. Cloth came from the cotton they grew. Cotton was spun into thread and thread wove into rough but serviceable clothing. The old women who made the clothing learned to put color into the material by crushing wild berries into water, then soaking the newly sown clothing in the brew. Their slaves were a colorful bunch who sang everywhere they went.

One morning Hershel came up on twenty-five rows of cotton that had been chopped. The stalks were ten to twelve inches high. Hershel saw something that made his heart skip a beat. For as far as he could see the cotton had been chopped down on just one row. Hershel followed the workers and as soon as he drew near, the row become whole again. Hershel could see the guilty one, so he called out, "Sully come here boy."

The young Negro was a sullied, light skinned slow moving boy. Hershel asked, "Why you chop all my cotton down on your row boy."

The strapping black said, "Don't know boss, maybe I confused."

Hershel said, "Well you get on back to the quarters now, I'll be long directly and we'll have us a talk, OK?"

Sully bobbed his head up and down, and walked away. Hershel told the two workers on either side of Sullie's row to catch it as they moved along. This was a first for Hershel. He figured he had lost a bail of cotton or more and he didn't know what to do about it. Hershel had never beaten one of his slaves, this one deserved a beating, but he didn't think he'd start now. These infractions did not happen that often, maybe he had been confused, and for sure he wasn't blessed with high intelligence

When Hershel arrived back home he went to the quarters to deal with Sully and found the boy in tears. The old women in the quarters were giving Sully a real rough time, after he came in bragging about what he had done. As Hershel stepped into the room he heard what they were saying. One was talking, she said, "You one dumb nigger boy. What you did, you need a hidden fo... In fact boy you make it harder on everyone, you dumb nigger!"

Hershel said, "That's enough. Sully, why did you chop my cotton down?"

Sully, through tears said," I guess I one Dumb Niger, don't beat me boss, I won chop no mo cotton down."

Hershel said," I don't beat my workers Sully but I'm really disappointed with you. I could sell you I suppose. You will work in the Plantation garden."

Old Gladys would keep Sully under an iron thumb and work his ass off, and if he gave old Gladys any smart talk, she would remove parts of his body he didn't really need to live and breathe with.

Things settled down on the plantation, the days were hot and long, the workers went to work early mornings and took a midafternoon break to lie around under shade trees. They went back to work late evenings and were home before dark. After the evening meal they sang for an hour or so. Hershel and Maisey would set on the back verandah and listen in contented silence.

CHAPTER 7

Sonny said, "The first sign of trouble came when sweet loveable Maisey turned cold in bed. She didn't just turn cold, she frosted up like a frozen pond of water in winter, and every time Hershel reached for her, she turned her back to him. The first time or two he thought well, "She's just tired that's all". Then weeks turned into a month then two. Finally; at wit's end; Hershel told Maisey they had to talk, now! Maisey sat down with folded hands and waited for him to say his piece, but wouldn't look him in the eye. Her head was bowed, as if in prayer. Hershel said, "We use to enjoy each other so much what happened. Why do you turn your back on me?"

Maisey began to cry but remained silent. After about thirty minutes of this, Hershel stomped out leaving Maisey crying at the table.

He was so frustrated, he threw himself into his work, and Maisey moved to one of the spare bed rooms off the kitchen and for sure, the one year marriage was in real trouble Sonny said, "After a time Hershel no longer attempted to talk to her. As a matter of fact, he gave up on her entirely. They lived in the same house, and that's all".

CHAPTER 8

At the end of August Hershel decided to take Maisey to the Doctor's down in Atlanta, and see what the matter was. This could not go on forever. When he approached her with his plan; she shouted at him, to stay out of her affairs, she wasn't sick, and didn't need a damn doctor!

Daulton ask at this point, "Was she pregnant?"

Sonny said, "I don't know, it's possible, but let me tell the rest of the story OK?"

The next day Hershel remained in bed for the first time in his adult life. He was just too miserable to get out of bed so he went back to sleep. When he woke up, the sun was high in the sky and the clock on the mantle showed 1016 AM. He was disgusted with himself. He quickly dressed and hurried to the kitchen for breakfast. The cook served him without comment, and disappeared. When alone, Hershel was about to put a fork of scrambled eggs into his mouth, when Maisey moaned from the spare bedroom off the kitchen. At first Hershel thought, Maisey might be sick, and then she moaned much louder. Hershel dropped his fork and bolted for his wife's room. He put his ear to the wood door and he knew what was happening. Someone was having sex in that room. He saw red; there was nothing wrong with her, she had cut him off because she had another lover. He ran to his den and grabbed his shotgun and two shells. He loaded the gun as he ran back to the bedroom. When he reached the door he simply kicked the damn thing off its hinges. There was the light skinned Negro Sully, rooting on his wife.They both jumped to their feet and stood there on the bed, stark fear in their eyes.

Hershel shot the Negro first, and then turned the gun on his wife. He still loved her, but had no choice but to pull the trigger. He shot her right between her beautiful breasts, and watched the light go out in her eye as she bounced off the wall. Then he sat down on the floor and cried like a baby. Lord how he must have loved that woman. He had taken the only option open to him."

Sonny said, "Daulton as you might guess, the bedroom was a bloody mess. Hershel got two of his most trusted blacks to assist him. He showed one where to dig the hole for the gun. Then him and the other one. Here Sonny's eyes misted up, and he said, "It was my own Granddaddy that helped Hershel bury the dead lovers in one common grave, somewhere way off on the back of the place. The two will never be found I'd bet you that."

Daulton set there thinking about Sonny's story. A customer came and went. He ask, "Sonny, how can Sally be that ghost's Grandchild, if Maisey and Hershel never had any children?" '

Sonny said, "Hershel remarried, and they had seven kids, one of them was your grandmother in law." Sonny and Daulton both found this funny, and had a good laugh.

CHAPTER 9

Daulton said, Wow. what a story. I can't wait to tell Sally!"

Sonny held both hands up, and said, "Whoa, maybe you should think this over Daulton. Why ruin your Wife's memories of her Granddaddy. Tell her, our search turned nothing up"

. Daulton said, "You're right, we will see."

Daulton drove home slowly, thinking about last night and today. Far out stuff. He made an attempt to give the gun to Sonny, but Sonny's eyes had grown to the size of walnuts and backing up, he said, "No suh, no suh not dis Negra man I scared dem ghost, don wont dem round hear."

The whites of his eyes were showing and he had reverted back to slave talk. Daulton got out of there before he busted a gut. He felt bad laughing at old Sonny, but the old man was comical.

When Dalton arrived back home Sally ask, "Well, what did you find out?"

Daulton said," not much Hon., maybe old sonny will still come up with something."

That was enough to satisfy her for now. She kissed him and jumped in her Honda and tore up the drive towards town.

After Sally left, Daulton grabbed a shovel and the gun, and headed for the garden. He dug a hole close to where he thought he found the piece and dropped the thing in and covered it up, then stomped it down and refilled the hole. He smoothed the dirt out, and as far as he was concerned, it was finished.

CHAPTER 10

Monday found Daulton at work at the Wynn Dixie over in Eufaula Alabama. He was the supervisor in the fruit and veggie department. He had been at work four hours when Sally called on her cell phone. She was frantic. She said, "Honey come home please, terrible things are happening! Come home now!"

Daulton told his assistant to take over; he had an emergency at home. Daulton broke the law all the way home. The only reason he didn't get a ticket was, the cop in Eufaula was busy out on the highway, writing some unlucky speeder a ticket, and Georgetown had dissolved their entire police force. Daulton pulled into his and Sally's drive and Daulton could already hear the unearthly sound. It sounded like demons in the movies. When Daulton opened his truck door, the sound multiplied by three. It was the most horrendous noise he had ever heard. He saw Sally in the dog pen. Her and their two Pit bulls were huddled together. Daulton thought, "Yeah, bad dogs my butt."

At that moment, a chair came through a window, almost bringing the entire frame along with it. Sally said, "Oh my God honey, something is destroying our home."

Daulton said, "I think a ghost is some kinda pissed off and we better stay out of its way. Let's not go near the house."

The rampage continued until the house had to be a total wreck inside. Then a mattress came flying through the same window. All at once it burst into flames. Daulton ran to his truck, grabbed his fire extinguisher and ran back and sprayed the mattress putting it out, but the damn thing burst into flames once more. Daulton dropped the empty extinguisher on the grass and told Sally to bring the dogs. They were getting the hell out of here. They all made a run for the pickup. The dogs made damn sure they beat both humans to the front seat, Daulton thought, "Oh my brave dogs." They were both down on the floor board shaking.

As Daulton backed up the driveway, the house began to vibrate and come apart, and then it went up in flames. They set there in a stupor and watched in horror as they become homeless.

The moral of this story is: be careful when you dig up the past. It may just come back and haunt you.

OTHER BOOKS PUBLISHED BY
THEODORE POTTER

THE SHIPLEYS

TRUE TALES OF ALASKA AND THEODORE
POTTER'S MEMIORS

GUNS, GOLD AND TRUE LOVE

WILDSTREAK

YOU'RE MOVING WHERE